PAJ

CW00815929

MAN©

Andrzej Griffith

This book is dedicated to
all my family and friends.

With a special dedication to
Jeanette

And to Jenny;
the girl I could not save.

A special thank you to Sarah
for your patience, understanding and motivation.

Thank you to Natasha and Sajjal
for great insight
while proof reading this book.

A final big thank you to Chutima Sangwarinta
For modelling so that I could finally get my cover.

The door shuts, and I am at home at last. Sanctuary, the centre of my world, my only refuge. I stagger over to the sink and drop the blood covered knife, creating a clattering sound of metal against metal, destroying the silence and shocking my senses into clarity once more. The boiling hot water scalds my hands as I try to scrub the blood off. I keep returning them to the hot water in a sporadic routine, cooling them off with cold water, each time removing more and more blood. Exhaustion finally takes over, it had threatened to catch up with me on my escape back home, but I was determined not to let it, my power of will would astound you, the grit and determination that I have whenever I set a task for myself. I could conquer the world in a day, if only I chose to do so.

I wipe my wet hands on the dirty dish-cloth, smearing the grimy white cloth turning it pink as the blood permeated through the rag. Afterwards I just flung it into some far away corner of the kitchen, for it to be forgotten. I just did not care anymore, there wouldn't be long left anyway. Slumping down in the dark blue chair in the living room, I gently sip the last bottle of beer from my fridge. There were six there this morning, and they all felt so good when I drank them down.

I was born in this chair, I felt that it was right that I should die in it too. Calm washes over me now, there is nothing left to do, nothing left to think. I will be dead soon, this is my last night alive. Sitting in the darkness, enjoying the complete silence around me, my eyes slowly close, and I am away...

The room around me means nothing, there are scattered beer bottles and pizza boxes by my feet. The leather chair that I am sitting on creaks with every movement, looking around I see nothing of importance, nor any hint or clue as to why I am here, there aren't any decorations or photographs in the flat, nothing to indicate that this is my home whatsoever. But then why would there be? There are no happy memories here.

I decide that the first thing I should do is take a shower, but I need to be careful I can't spend too long on any one task, it is good to enjoy the luxuries of life, but my time is precious, and it can't be mismanaged, especially not on a frivolous task such as washing, not when there is so much to do.

There is still blood on my hands. I was born with blood on my hands. I sigh deeply, very deeply, deeper than you could ever manage in your meaningless life. Why hadn't he washed his hands? My hands, they are my hands now – but they are still carrying his guilt. I feel exasperated, he must have been a deep and powerful man, someone I could never be, and someone I would not like to cross. At least he was dead now, and whoever he killed, I know they deserved it.

I can't cook pancakes for breakfast, I have a craving for pancakes, and I can't make any, there are no eggs, no flour, there is no milk, not even simple pancake mix, this really irked me. There isn't any food anywhere in the flat. Not even an apple or a single solitary biscuit, every cupboard is completely bare, this flat might as well be part of a movie set, or a museum display for all its barrenness, although why a slum would be in a museum I do not know.

Outside I go to the nearest diner and order breakfast, and only pancakes will do. After settling for two servings, I decide to order a coffee as well. I've been sitting by the window, watching people go by. Instinct has led me to keep my head down, not to make small talk, avoid people whenever I can and to display a cold front to everyone. But sitting next to the window, I don't have to keep my head down, or distance myself from people, I can just watch them pass by. After half an hour I have been inspired to go to the park, I haven't just been watching people with a distant gaze as one would watch a fish tank, I have been studying them as you would look through a catalogue. I have been watching them to search for ideas on what to do. Inspiration did not come straight away, only the idea of where to get inspiration from; the park.

After watching shoppers, students, diners, commuters going to work, I eventually saw a jogger; out of place on the busy sidewalk, but at least I knew where to go. I had no interest in shopping, or going to watch a movie, the arcades, bowling alleys and pool halls were all to be avoided, I wanted to be outdoors, basking in the sunshine, and doing something new.
A short stroll later and I was there, ah, this was much better, I could see a kite flying, dogs being walked, a child learning to ride his bike with his parents and older brother, a sheer look of concentration on his face, looking straight down at the front wheel, not even seeing the huge smile on his Fathers face, or hearing his Mother clapping with joy.
A group of students were kicking a football around, there was so much going on. I just had to find a bench somewhere and wait until I saw exactly what I was after.

Forty minutes later, after finding a decent sport shop nearby, and after returning to the park, there I was rushing around on a pair of brand new roller skates. Grinning like an idiot, and falling every time I tried to use my skates to walk in, I felt like a new born calf standing on ice. I didn't care how I looked, I was having a great time. It wasn't easy to find a pair of roller skates, after trying on a pair of rollerblades, I found them unbearably uncomfortable on my ankles. Many of the shop clerks looked too young to have ever tried on a pair of roller skates, and I suppose that they would have been as foreign to them as rollerblades were to me.

I spent all day in the park, I loved it here, I didn't need to explore the rest of New York, this was my world right here; the birds, the trees, the sunshine, why would I want to be anywhere else, when everything that would make me happy was all around me.

I visited a Starbucks for a coffee, I had spent about ten minutes outside the coffee shop, trying to outweigh the pro's and con's of taking off my roller skates. I had been determined to keep them on all day, right up till I got home, I had successfully manoeuvred my way from the park and along the sidewalks, even managing to cross the street without getting myself killed. The bookstore had been interesting, I received many strange looks, and I was relieved to find out that they had an elevator, I doubt that I would have managed the stairs, I think that I would have been unable to stop laughing as I hung on to the banisters for dear life. The girl who served me behind the counter had found it amusing, her smile was nice to see in a sea of sneers and contempt. Sometimes a single smile can turn your day around, and when all you have is one day, that smile is magnified to mean so much more.

So I now had two options, I could keep my roller skates on and struggle to get served, find a seat and get to it in time without burning myself, or even worse losing my balance and finding myself sprawled across someone else's table, scalding them as I fell, or on the other hand I might be refused service for going into Starbucks with only socks on my feet, and after skating all day, I don't want to know what my feet will smell like, maybe the hygiene factor won't come into it, maybe it is only an issue if I am on the serving side of the counter, well if I do get served, I'll drink my coffee outside.

No one even noticed, perhaps the counter was too high, or the staff to busy, they were working at a frantic pace, and the whole time I was standing in the queue I found myself wondering why there were so many of them, how could they justify their jobs by doing so little? I received my coffee after my order had been passed down the lines through the hands of six people, wondering all the time how they had managed to get my order right, didn't Chinese whispers always have the opposite affect? I found myself glad that I was not working there, having to shout out and repeat everything that was shouted at me, and in turn hear that being repeated further down the line, perhaps people have become so incompetent in their skills, that this autonomous structure is the only way to ensure that work was carried out correctly.

Flower

The night closed in around me, I felt uneasy as it did so. I could feel my life ending, time slipping away as my eyelids grew heavier and heavier. I had enjoyed my life, and I wished the next one to take my place all the best with his. He would replace me soon, I would be gone and he would wake in my place.

Today was the day that was going to change everything, I wouldn't know it yet, but my actions over the next few hours would have dire consequences, and everlasting repercussions, only, I would not be around to see them. I would be the catalyst to set things in motion, and all the others who would follow after me would remember me for what I did this day, it would be up to them to pick up the pieces.

If only I'd have had more time, I could have paved the way for the rest of them, left more information on what happened that night, why I did what I did. Although the rest would have done the same in my place, so would all those that had lived and died before me, I was sure of it, I had to be, for I was cursing the rest of those to come with my burden.

The whole day had been mine, nothing of particular interest had occurred, nothing of note to anyone who had a lifetime to live their dreams anyway, but in my short one day life I felt I had gazed at wonderment at my world, before it was destroyed forever as I would be plucked cruelly from it, having had a brief taste of honey and nothing more. One day, a single day to live, it really infuriated me, did any other creature simply live for one day? I didn't know, but what I did know was all those I saw around me today, didn't live their lives to their fullest extent, had I been given their lives, I would have made every moment count, not for a day as I did now, but for a lifetime.

One of the few advantages of having to share one body, one space, is that although we do not share memories we do share each other's knowledge, so when I was walking home, even though I had not walked through that part of the city earlier in the day, I was able to know a faster route home, thanks to one of us having previously walked the same streets, long before I had arrived for my given day. Cutting a shorter route home, I passed through the back streets of Chinatown, there were still puddles on the ground from the morning rain, and as I was trampling over sodden cardboard and manoeuvring around wooden fruit crates, a women's accent called out to me.

'Hey mister, you want girlfriend?'

And I thought, why not? I was a virgin after all, my libido wasn't particularly excitable, nor was sex anything I had really thought about during my day either, but walking home, all I was going to do was sit in my chair drinking beer and waiting for the night to come and swallow me whole.

The mama-san led me throughout the dingy alleyway entrance, I hadn't even seen her standing there, smoking her cigarette, was this the back entrance, was she on a cigarette break when she saw me? Or was that the only entrance that I had just walked through? The Mama-san was a short plump woman in her late forty's, raven black hair, frizzy and out of shape, reaching her shoulders, she had fat chubby cheeks, pockmarked with blemishes and acne scars. Everything she wore was black, from her leather skirt that was too tight to the wafer thin long sleeved jumper that had been stretched out of shape and had lost its elasticity with age. I should have negotiated a price, or asked a few questions before entering the brothel, so that I would know what to expect, but when you only live one day, price is not an option, and details are left by the wayside.

I don't know what was supposed to happen next, the Mama-san never got the chance to lead me to my room, or to take me to where the girls were waiting for me to choose one of them. I was still following behind her when I heard the tears. I had heard raised voices, and shouting in Chinese coming from a few of the rooms on the ground floor, but during a lull in the noise I heard a sob, and a jolt of cold ice shot down my spine. I could sense something was not right, so I started opening doors left, right and centre, rushing from room to room as fast as I could, ignoring the startled faces, the shouting of the Mama-san, the gasps of the girls, until I came to one room, an office of sorts, filing cabinet in the corner, a desk next to the door I had opened, and there lying in the floor, crawling to the corner of the room was a Chinese girl, her hair was hanging over her face, and I could see her shoulder blades sliding past each other as she slowly dragged herself deeper into the corner, her arm shacking with the adrenaline of someone who had just been beaten. And that was it, my brain was taking over, like a chess-player who knows what he is doing five moves ahead. Without looking I reached behind me, gripping the Mama-sans neck tight with my right hand, crushing her windpipe, the whole time staring down at the three Chinese men who stood before me, they wouldn't be standing for long. Letting her body fall to the ground I heard her head fall against the wall as she slumped down dead. I closed the door to the hall that we had come through, there was no need to lock it, no one would get past me, and right there I beat those men to death first with my hands, then I took advantage of the chair that was next to me, pulling it from under the desk by my side. I beat them without remorse, without showing any sign of emotion on my face, and I beat their bodies long after they were dead. The only other door in the office looked like a inner door to a safe that you might see in an old-fashioned bank, black bars and a heavy square lock next to the door handle, and between the gaps in the bars in a room no bigger than a New York bathroom were girls who were so scared that they had retreated deep within themselves, you could see it in their eyes, the pupils were so small and black, shrunken to help distance their mind from the horror of where their bodies were. They didn't fear me, neither did they feel scared when they saw the deaths of four of their captors, for them all fear was the same, nothing could worsen the hell that they were already living through.

I left the girl in the corner, I had work to do, and moving from room to room I killed all the men I could find, with the simple justification that any men there were regulars, and knew that the girls were forced into doing what they did. Anyone who might have been new to the brothel should have sensed the girls fear, the tension in their bodies, their movements jerky and staccato, blank faces, tears and forced smiles. Anyone seeing this should have walked out, anyone left was guilty, and in my eyes the customers were as bad as the pimps and gangsters, all would die. I had gathered together five other girls, having gone from room to room, the night was going past me in a blur, but now that I was certain that every room had been searched I was beginning to calm down, I still looked the same on the surface, stone faced and steely eyed, and on the inside my heart rate slowed, the red mist before my eyes lowered, and I began to hear the smaller sounds around me, the breathing of the girls, the ticking clock, the click of the door handle as it turned and released, and then I ushered the five girls into the office. The silence was astounding, now that my crazed behaviour was over, the behaviour of the girls that were being held captive was eerie. There were no screams to accompany the four corpses on the office floor, no tears or gasps or wails or cries of rage. Retrieving a key, even as I held it in my hand I could not remember how I had acquired it or where I had gotten it from, which body was it found on? Or was it in the desk drawer? I had to keep a grasp of my reality, I still had time to get home before I died, no one had ever died outside the apartment before, or not as far as I knew, I found myself beginning to wonder what would happen? Would it be dangerous to die outside the safety of the apartment? Would the next one remember how to get back? Would there be a next one to take over?

Opening the filing cabinet, I found a bundle of passports, all of them red. A pile of documents, carbon copies of people's lives, the keys to their freedom. I wondered why they were locked in the filing cabinet and not the desk drawer, perhaps the lock was better, did it matter? I needed to keep my focus. There was nothing of interest in the desk, nothing useful anyway, searching the bodies I took all the cash I could from those that I had killed. After opening the cage door, I handed out the passports to each girl in silence, stopping to read their names before doing so, I don't know why I did this, but I felt that it was perhaps to know the names of those I had helped. I also shared out all the cash that I had gathered together, including all of my own, after all I would not need it anymore, and the next one to come tomorrow...well I am sure he would understand. Thinking that those few measly dollars would not be enough between all the girls, after all there were thirteen of them, the five I rescued from upstairs and along the corridors of the brothel the seven locked up and lying nearly on top of each other in the squalor and filth of that makeshift dungeon, and the girl who's cries originally alerted me to what was going on. I headed back to the two men that I had killed, clients that I had come across in two separate rooms near the entrance, I took the time to go through their possessions, taking their wallets, watches, gold chains and rings then returned to the office I began sharing all that I had gathered together to the stunned and silenced girls. Afterwards I headed upstairs to do the same thing, searching for money and possessions, taking whatever I could from the bloodied bodies, thinking of how much of a shame it was that I had not arrived during a busier time, I could have killed so many more.

When I got back down the stairs, all the girls had gone, I don't know why I was surprised, the must have thought that when I left the office the second time that I had gone for good, and following my example they must have slipped out quietly, did they go together I wonder? Or did they run off scarred as soon as they reached the street, terrified and alone, with nowhere to go, or any idea what to do next. My only blessing was that I was able to give out all the passports, there had been none left, meaning that there weren't any other girls held against their will in another building somewhere in the city, or perhaps in another city altogether. Neither were there any girls left over, I would have hated to see the look on a young girls face as she realised that her passport was not with all the others.

I had thought of burning the whole building down, I didn't care what happened to the neighbouring buildings, let their neighbours burn as well, especially if they knew what was going on. But then I decided to let the police see their faces, they can find their ID's in their wallets, each one open and placed on their chests.

I had Just stepping outside, back into the dark alley that I had begun travelling through on my way home, when suddenly a voice behind me calls out; 'Where I go now? I come with you, we go from here.' It was the girl who had been beaten, the one who had slowly crawled into the corner, trying to get away from her abusers. I looked around the alleyway; all the other girls had disappeared, I wondered why she had hung around? Had she waited for me to come out? Or had she just been unsure of where to go next and what to do, when I stumbled back out and across her path? There was nothing for it now apart from to make my way home, if she wanted to follow she could, it's her business what she does now, whether or not I'd let her in once I got back to the flat would be another matter.

Back at the flat it was a relief to see that it was only eleven o'clock, that didn't leave me much time, but it might still be enough. Turning around, the door of the apartment open, the Chinese girl was still stood in the hallway outside, her head peering in, like a fox, nervous to enter a barn, sticking its head in cautiously before dashing in. Having urged her to come in, and to close the door behind her, I turned to go to the kitchen, she must have been hungry, I couldn't offer her much, but I wanted her to feel safe here, even if it might be for only one night.

However I had a plan, I just had to plan it out carefully to make sure that it will work, it was a cunning idea, but

I have to make sure it lasts, it can't be a flash in the pan, it has to have; what's that word...ah yes, durability.

After a few minutes of pottering around in the kitchen, bathroom and bedroom, I returned to find the girl still standing in the living room, I ushered her to sit down, she was beginning to make me nervous by just standing there on the spot. I placed a sandwich in front of her; it was crudely made with wafer thin white bread, and a glass of orange juice, the only real source of any nutrients in the whole apartment. As she tucked in, I placed a t-shirt and some jeans on the arm of her chair, 'I don't have any clothes that will fit you, but you can have these until something better comes along.' Looking into her face, I no longer saw someone who was scared, merely someone who looked very annoyed. 'What's your name?' She had to have a name, and I knew she could speak English, I had to call her something after all, even if it was only for a few more minutes.

'My name Flower' she turned away from her sandwich to look up at me now, her round cheeks, dishevelled hair that had been partly dyed brown, giving a two layered affect with the black roots showing through, and as she faced you the hair underneath the top layer was still dark and black, making her face stand out, but still seeming dark and broody as if her eyes were glaring at you from a cave.

'But that's not your real name, I didn't see a 'Flower' on any of the passports. 'My Chinese name is Li Yilin, but call me Flower, or Yilin, or anything you want.'

'Anything I want, how can you say a thing like that? Your name is something unique to you, how can you be so flippant about it.' I decided to calm down, I didn't want to shock her, especially after the night she had had. I was just feeling weary that was all, I had better

17

explain things to Flower, before it became too late. I showed her the bedroom, and explained that it was now hers, for as long as she wanted to stay here. We talked about how she had arrived here, and how she had ended up where she did.

Her cousin was the manager of a Chinese restaurant, and had worked profusely to allow her to come over on a visa, however after only three months in the city, Flowers cousin had had to return home, due to her mother's illness. Another manager had taken over, and Flower was promised another job as a waitress in a sister restaurant, but knowing no one in the city, she was easily taken advantage of, after having moved out of her cousins apartment, she was promised a room above her new restaurant, but neither the job nor the restaurant existed. The new manager of the restaurant had sold her to the triads, knowing that she was alone in the city, and that no one would ever find her out. Her possessions were taken to the brothel, where Flower had been beaten and abused, until her captors thought she would be too scared or unable to run away. After being beaten and ridiculed, she described the actions of both the men and the women of the brothel, how they beat her, spat on her and humiliated her. The first night after they had beaten her, they pushed her to the floor, keeping her there, pushing her down, keeping her down, under the soles of their shoes as they laughed, the Mama-san tearing at her clothes, scratching her and slapping her, always on her backside or across her chest, as if to try to reveal her underwear and her skin underneath her clothing, she had worn her best suit, hoping to impress the manager on the first night, but they had taken her to the brothel, not to a restaurant, and now her suit was filthy and torn . The abuse would stop once she was thrown back into the locked room, some of the other girls had tried to comfort her, they had all been Chinese, but not all of them spoke Mandarin, there were Cantonese speaking girls there as well, and Flower had been the only girl who could also speak English. Some of the girls had shied away from her, and some didn't seem bothered by the abuse, having become so disjointed from their surroundings, preferring to sit motionless, in a semi-comatose state, they must have become numb from all the horrors they were put through, some girls had tried to persuade her that it was easier to just let go, give in, let them take her. But Flower knew that once the beatings would stop, if she had given in to them, they would wait for the bruises to clear up, and then the real abuse would begin, and she would die on the inside. Luckily for her, the same day that she had been brought to and locked up in the brothel, she had witnessed the murder of her captors, and her subsequent release.

The hardest part of the night should have been explaining to her that when I went to sleep at around midnight, I would die, and someone else would wake up living in my body in the morning. I'd never had to explain that the curious thing that happens to my body on a daily basis before to anybody. You can't make friends in a day, perhaps some others had, meeting someone in a bar, drinking, eating and getting along well with a group of strangers, only to die that night, and the memory of their meeting would vanish, and besides which other one of us would want to meet someone else's friends, to meet a group of strangers again, to pretend to know them, to feign interest, why would one of us waste our precious time like that?
The language barrier held back our conversation, she could explain herself, but not fully. She understood

everything I said, but I could see the look of frustration on her face as the words she used were holding her back in trying to convey what she wanted to say. I hoped I wasn't scaring her, but not being able to control what the next one would do once he was born, I had to warn her, to prepare her.

She seemed very doubtful about what I was telling her, looking at me like I was mocking her, taking advantage of her lack of understanding, in the typical way that most people treat foreigners. Well, come the morning she would see, I knew one thing for certain, I may have been born into this body, but I was not here when this body first came into this world, I began to feel a slight sadness for the others who had shared this body before me but were too young to experience the wonders of life, at least that would be better than the fate of those to come later on; to be young and full of life and vigour, but trapped in an old body, unable to escape its limitations, that would be a prison, for a day, a prison for a lifetime, continued over and over for all those unfortunate souls, the victims of circumstance, thinking if only they had had their day in the sun sooner.

I spent my remaining time putting my plan into motion, I was sure it would work, it had to. I just hope that everything would work out for Flower, I felt bad that I could do nothing else for her, but if I couldn't be someone to guide her through her troubled life, at least I was able to set her free. I handed her all the money I had left in my wallet, wished her luck, and gave her a hug goodnight, I held her for a while, patting my hand against her back, and then I walked over to the dark blue living room chair that took its place in the centre of the room, and fell asleep, letting death engulf me.

We woke, but something was different, there was a different feeling, like a ripple in a pool of water, spreading its effect to the whole pool. Something must have happened, something someone did before, but will affect us. Looking around our home, we spied a note on the table next to me, our stomach suddenly lurched, one that had gone before had left a message for us, the message was new, so it must have been the one that lived in this body yesterday, oh dear, it had to be important then. We almost didn't want to look, but knew that we must, for there was a strange pact that existed between all those that shared this body. The note read as thus...

'This is your mission, Flower is the Chinese girl in your apartment, she needs our help, not just yours and mine – and as you can tell from the note I am no longer able to help her! But all of our help.

She's in danger, so you must protect her.

She has nowhere to live, so you must let her live here.

No harm or distress, physical, mental or otherwise can ever come to her.

Her life while she is living here or otherwise must be made comfortable, get her what she needs.
And the final point scrawled on the note was;

'Be patient with her.'

The note continued; 'We have adopted her, so she is now our responsibility, look upon her as your adopted sister. You can't run away from your responsibility.

We have to do the right thing. She is the only one who knows about us, she also knows the rules on this note, so you can't destroy it or hide it from her. This is our mission in life, Flower is our mission, our reason for living now.

We did not like the sound of this at all, what were we expected to do? How old is this 'Flower' anyway, five, six years old? we gently got up from the chair, the leather creaking as we did so, slowly turning around, as if there were a wolf in here with us, we saw her huddled in the kitchen chair, next to the fridge, her feet brought up onto the seat, her hair hanging over the front of her face, and with her arms wrapped around her legs, there was the biggest kitchen knife we had ever seen.

Was that our knife? Well I suppose it must have been, we can't imagine she'd go out to specially buy a kitchen knife...or would she? we didn't know this girl after all.

What do we do next? She wasn't asleep, we could see one eye looking at us through her hair. But she wasn't moving, not even a stir, just the tip of the knife swaying gently, as if in a breeze.

'Eh...so your Flower then? Well I don't know how or why your here, but I can bet you haven't had breakfast yet, you can tell me what this is all about over breakfast, and then maybe you can begin to tell me what I need to do for you.'

She followed us out of the flat, that was a good sign, she brought the kitchen knife with her – wrapped in a man's coat, that was not a good sign. She hadn't spoken to us yet, but seemed content to cross the street with us to a nearby diner. We sat opposite each other in a booth and ordered our breakfasts. We was glad when we heard her speak English, we had wondered whether or not she was able to speak English.

Halfway through our scrambled eggs, Flower looked up and ended the awkward silence between us.

'Why you so quiet today, last night you no stop talking. Crazy man.'

This did make us blink, we were really confused, and didn't know what to do about the situation we were in. 'Last night? I didn't meet you until this morning, I wasn't even alive last night.' Flower swayed her head from side to side, as if to look at me independently with one eye at a time. 'So it true den, what you say last night, you die, you come back, every day - new life. So nice, so lucky I want to be cat like you, new life every time you want it. Maybe it good time for you to have new life, after all dat killing you do yesterday, you could use new start.' That's when we froze. That's when we realised that we had inherited more than just Flower and her troubles, we had inherited all of yesterdays troubles as well. But could she be serious, she just sat there chewing on a piece of her crust, and swirling the straw in her milkshake nonchalantly. Did she really say what she said? Did she mean it, or was she teasing us because we had no memory of what all the others had done, does she know this, does she do this every day to amuse herself, teasing each and every one of us?

We decided to go for the direct approach, all of us are nervous and shy by nature, and Flower was making us feel even more so. If we only have one day each, we don't want to retreat further into ourselves, the sooner we can help her, the sooner we can have the rest of the day to ourselves.

'Look, what do you need. I mean what can I do for you, I was told to help you, so ... what's the first thing, the most important thing I can do to help you?' And for the first time, she made me really notice her. 'I need clothes, have to go shopping, I wear mans cloths, no good, too big, clothes he gave me yesterday, not you, other you. I know you no kill, no have killer's eyes, you different today. So you tell truth, new soul in your body. I like you, I like mysterious. Yesterday you save me, I like you forever. You change every day, I like new you forever. ' And with that she smiled, a beautiful smile, I could see the real her, beneath the greasy dishevelled hair, his clothes, hers now, he won't be back for them. Her face slowly peeled away, all those layers; dirt, grit, grime, distrust, fear, anger, I could see her, the real her – and her face was beautiful.

So we went shopping. Shopping can be one of two things, boring or exciting, not your own shopping of course, but boyfriends the world over will know what we am talking about, you either have the patience of a saint and the fashion advice of a designer, or you are bored stiff to the point where...well everyman knows what's running through his mind while he waits for hours on end, holding his girlfriends coat outside of the changing rooms.

Shopping with Flower was different, she was embarrassing. She tripped over while she tried on clothing, preferring to change in the isles rather than the changing rooms, wanting to know our opinion as she was trying things on, rather than having to ferry back and forth past the draped curtains. As we watched her even now, trying to put a blue shoe on her foot, the other wearing a different, colour, make and style of shoe altogether, she tripped forwards, then stumbled backwards, before losing her balance altogether and falling heavy on her knee, the blue stiletto still only half on. 'Agh, I bruise my hip on dis thing here.' And she turned to hit a metal arm where shirts were hung. 'And graze my knee now doing same ting.' we had tried to offer our advice of actually going to get a shop clerk to bring a pair of shoes , where they would both be the same, and of a size that would actually fit, and not cause her to injure herself in the art of changing. There was an air of hopelessness around her while she shopped, she couldn't try a bracelet on her wrist without breaking it as she tried to take it off. She was a wonder to watch, this was better than going to the zoo.

One thing she did insist on though was her underwear. She had to show it off. To begin with we thought she was just dressed shabbily, having bought a pair of Jeans that were too big for her, or too tight, we could not work out the confusion that was a woman's anatomy. The Jeans hung too low, showing way too much of her backside, but they were tight around her legs, and wouldn't even reach her shoes, instead ending somewhere on her shins, somewhere north of her ankles. Were they too loose to stay up, or altogether too tiny to conceal everywhere you were paying them to? We asked her about them, well we had to, she was embarrassing enough as it was – we thought we were helping.

'No, my hips supposed to be showing, dis way you can see, good huh?' That was the problem, we didn't understand. The 'hips' seemed to refer to everything lower than the ribs but above the knees, which now colourfully included the new bruise on her back and her visible black thong. 'But I only show half, must hide something...', and as her eyes rolled up into her head, the word that she was thinking of emerged, 'for imagination.' And she was totally serious. 'Flower, you don't leave anything to the imagination, your clothes can't get any tighter, and one half of your underwear strap is pulled up so high over your jeans it looks like you got dressed while fleeing a burning building.'

'Hey, dis my way, this who I am, you no like I don't care. He didn't judge me. Like butterfly he let me open my wings and show true colours. You no hold me back, you no right to hold me back...have no right to hold me back, understand?'

*

Looking up from the note in my hand, Flower was eating a breakfast of burnt toast and jam, there were two cups of coffee on the kitchen table, she had made me a cup, before I had even come into this world. 'So how long have you been living here?' I was hoping that I wasn't asking her any questions that she had been asked too often already. 'One week, since he save me. Killed nine (unclarified Chinese word) to save me and many others. But I fine now, other girls I don't know, not know what happen to them, not know where they are now. They should have waited like me, good life here with you.' Well she seemed to be really comfortable here in the apartment. Just looking at the kitchen table, it could have been the breadboard of her life, such was the tapestry of crumbs all over it. Was that the work of a week's worth of easting toast? Or was that just the result of a mornings session of eating toast? I doubted very much that if I had turned the toaster upside down over the table in an attempt to loosen a jammed piece of crust, the end result of the way the table would look, would still be a great deal tidier than it was now. As we talked about the days events, what we were going to do, what she wanted to do, what I really wanted to do, I kept asking her about her week living here, how had the others been, how had they acted towards her, were they kind, did they all act the same? Did she have to cower and hide some days, only to go out to central park to fly a kite in a carefree way the next day? Did she fear the mornings, not knowing who would wake up in this body? Naturally the one she talked about the most was the one who had saved her, she kept going back to him time and time again, even though he was the one that she had known for the shortest time, in fact she had only met him during his swan-song, as he did not have much time left before he was about to die. I was horrified to discover that on that night, they had walked back here together, him covered in blood, his t-shirt and face were splattered with it, his hair all matted and wild. I subconsciously rubbed my hands over my shaved head, how long had it been shaved now? Should I shave it as well? Will there be routines now that each of us have to do regardless, like shaving our heads, one uniformed haircut for all of us? Apparently she had looked no better, her face battered and bruised, her top was torn, revealing a part of her bra, and her nosebleed had dribbled down her front, far enough even to ruin her jeans. What a way to go home what a way to get caught, of course he would have been fine, it's the next one that would have woken up in a cell. A shiver ran down my spine, I could have woken up today in prison. With that thought I suddenly grabbed her arm, we were going out, we were going to begin enjoying the day right now.

For me every meal was a new revelation, but I was beginning to wonder what Flower was making of all this. Did she see the same person eating the same three meals every day, but pretending that each time was the first? Was I simply just forgetting the previous day, didn't my memory last from one morning until the next? Or was I just losing my mind? Perhaps even my doubts were a daily occurrence. But where had I come from? Had there been a time when this body had not been shared? Was there a time when someone normal lived in this body, was I ever normal?

Flower had made herself really comfortable in the flat, the place was a lot cleaner, than when she had arrived, and probably more than it had ever been. She did not know if the flat belonged to him, or if he was just renting it. There was so much that she didn't know about him. But she felt comfortable in his presence, and every day was a new adventure, for her as well as for him. She just liked trailing in his wake, to see what he would do next.

She busied herself while he slept, cleaning the kitchen, washing his clothes, although he only had two pairs of jeans and three t-shirts. His only jewellery was his watch. There was nothing in the apartment that actually belonged to him, nothing personal anyway, only general things. No photographs, diary, calendar, no form of any identification anywhere, no mail came to the house, and although Flower had asked him his name on a daily basis, he had only answered with silence, but it was much deeper than that, his eyes would glaze over, his lips parting slightly, and you could tell he was far away, the next moment he would snap out of it forgetting that the question was even asked.

Flower had gone with him for breakfast in only three different diners and coffee shops, none of the cashiers or waiters and waitresses knew him, in the corner shop no one recognised him, anywhere they went, there wasn't anybody that called him by his name. Flower

28

had never seen her neighbours, there was no phone in the apartment, and he never went anywhere to check his e-mails either. The mailbox that belonged to him had no name on it, he might have been a phantom, a ghost, just a made up fictional man who came to save her. She might wake up, and still be held in that brothel, a sex slave being beaten and abused, and no one even knowing she was there.

Who was this man, this walking mystery? Where did he come from? He didn't have a strong accent of any kind. Flower hadn't been out of China long enough to be able to tell the differences in the English accent well enough to place a person's nationality or origin. But she had noticed that he definitely did not have the drawl and twang of a New Yorker. How did he get here, and how did he get lost here? Why was it that he was left behind?

One unusual morning he had woken with the dawn, nearly at the same time as Flower, as they shared a breakfast together, the scarlet light of day shining through the blinds, they just sat in silence, letting the sunlight of the coming day illuminate the room, changing the colour of the glow, minute by minute.

Hidden in some dark corner, Flower had come across a pair of roller skates. With a perplexed look on her face she turned to him and said 'I not know where these come from, I clean this place many time, but never find them before, maybe I need clean better.' No matter how dishevelled her clothes are or how obscure her choice of a frizzy hairstyle is, you could never beat the smile on her face. Even though the roller skates were clearly meant for a man, that wasn't going to deter Flower from wearing them, she even had to take them off again in order to stuff socks down the front , all the way to the toes so that they would fit her properly. She did not bother to think that she still couldn't use them, let alone keep her balance in them.

So there she was, in the kitchen of all places, holding on to anything within reach, unable to even stand up properly, she was a sore sight, she might have well been trying to walk on ice, her skates were sliding everywhere, and she was making it increasingly difficult to take her seriously, the more she fell and leant over, the more she showed off her thong. There was one constant about Flower that he had noticed, it was the fact that he would always be embarrassed by the more revealing and colourful aspect of her appearance. Flower had began to get the hang of the skates, she was able to move around, using only the freezer door and sink to hold on to, instead of anything within reach. She was also upright, and hadn't had to manoeuvre by placing her hands or knees on the floor for a while. Brushing a stray wisp of hair out of her eyes, she said 'Inside too dangerous, much better if we go outside, you want we go to the park?'

After scowling at me when I suggested that she take off the skates and carry them, if not all the way to the park, then at least while we went down stairs, I was getting the feeling that Flower was getting a second childhood, for today at least, I knew she would blatantly refuse to take the skates off, so as a compromise I gave her a piggy-back down the stairs, carrying her, and trying not to trip or fall, dreading the thought that the both of us would end up in a broken heap at the bottom of the stairs. This filled her with joy, I felt like I was her little pet, especially after we went outside and she asked me in what she thought must have been a cute way, to carry her as she was, all the way to the park. I was sure that if I looked over my shoulder as she asked me, she would have had puppy dog eyes to match the pouting face that she would inevitably be making. I never cared what people thought of me, I wouldn't be around long enough to care, a shaved head does tend to give the wrong impression, and by the state of my wardrobe, none of the others had ever cared for personal appearance, at least that's what I found out by the shabby and stained clothing that I had at my disposal. Perhaps I should take a page out of Flowers book, and smarten myself up a little, take some personal pride in myself, and at least leave some decent clothes for the others that would come after me. Flower was exactly the same, she put a lot of pride in her appearance, she looked the way she wanted to look, but the fact that her thong was always on public display, and according to her, today was the first time that the top of her bra was also visible, she was going for a new look apparently, but I suspected that she was lying about this. We drew a lot of attention, a skinhead in a white vest walking down the street with a Chinese girl wearing roller skates on his back, I knew that Flower would be revealing herself more than usual, so I decided to ask her if she minded.

'No, they can see my hips all the time, today, special, they can see even more.' And then she began to giggle like a little girl.

I was so relieved to finally reach Central Park, Flower may have been Asian but she was heavy, in fact she seemed to be the complete opposite of her name, she wasn't delicate, pretty or refined, and she certainly wouldn't inspire you towards writing poetry about her.
I wondered if any of the others had ever jokingly began calling her Weed instead of Flower. I parked myself on

the nearest bench as soon as Flower jumped down from my back, she was eager to be off enjoying herself, and off she went, waving as she tried to pick up her stride. Sitting there watching her skate, making sure no one else got too near to her, I felt so possessive about her, not jealous but protective, I didn't want anyone to bump into her, or to say anything spiteful about her, I wouldn't even tolerate a bad look in her direction. I was scared that she was too fragile after everything that she had been through, and look at her now, not a care in the world. Maybe the old her died as well and she has also been born again, without memory and without any cares or troubles. I had to protect her now, but I was scared of drowning her, smothering her with my protection. I did not want to clip her wings, never letting her fly again, to crush her like a child trying to catch a butterfly, too eager but discovering that in the pursuit of trying to catch beauty, you have killed beauty, as the butterfly lies crushed when your hands open up, something precious lost forever.

*

It had been a wonderful day, Flower was really pleased, she had gone out to the park with him, they had had a glorious day weather wise, and now they were both sat together on the bench, contemplating their thoughts and watching the world go by. Flower had been having so much fun on his skates, they weren't ideal f course, being too big and bulky for her had meant that she had fallen a lot more often than usual, and being as clumsy as she was, even with the right skates, she still would have fallen over a great deal.

Central Park was vast, and it never lost its charm. Flower liked bringing him here, to sit beneath the trees, watching people go by. It had a calming effect on him. Flower had only been up to the Empire states Building on one occasion, it was a rainy Thursday afternoon about a week ago, and she had marvelled at the city beneath her, the sheer size of it, and there she was on top of the world. Time and time again as the two of them had walked around the observation deck, Flower had kept returning to look at Central Park, a true Jewel in the city, with buildings bordering high on every side of the park, Flower thought that the developers must have been desperate to build over the park, as the city had grown over the years, how had the Park survived under so much pressure, how was it not lost under the strain of the human ant hive. Flower was glad that it was still here in her lifetime, for her to see and enjoy, and would pity future generations that would wonder at old photographs, looking in disbelief at the green heart of the city that had been lost hundreds of years ago.

Sitting side by side on the green, metal bench, under the shade of an oak tree, Flower had taken off her skates in order to rest her feet, the grass felt good as she curled and uncurled her toes, tearing at the small blades of grass as she did so. After a lengthy silence, with the sun shining on their faces, Flower turned to him, and asked a question that she should have asked sooner, but it had never dawned on her to do so until now, all the times she had been to the park, she had never thought to ask before, but sitting there now, watching fathers play with sons, mothers walking with prams, families having picnics, why had the obvious been right in front of her all this time, yet she had not noticed it!

'Do you have any family? I never asked before, but do you know if you have any brothers or sisters anywhere? Or anyone else, can you remember anyone? Are your parents still alive?' It had taken a while before Flower had asked him this question, once she knew that she had to ask, she had taken the time to compose herself, and had been able to ask him, using what she believes was the correct English. She already knew the answer, but wanted to ask, just in case it sparked a memory, or something else, something deeper, she had to try, she so desperately wanted to help him, to try and get him to help himself.

After a few moments, he did answer, but he had to think about it first, perhaps, just like her, he had never thought about it before, or not for a while anyway.

Rubbing his hands over the short bristles of his shaved head, he sat back, leaning against the back of the bench. 'No, I don't think I have any family, none that I know of anyway, and I am pretty sure that none of the others ever found or heard from a brother or sister or any other family member, or I'm sure they would have written about it, like they wrote about you. Anyway, I have you don't I.' And with that he winked at Flower, making her smile, showing all of her teeth as she did so. 'Your my sister now, I'll be fine as long as I have you to look out for.' He reached over with his right hand, to stroke the hair at the back of her head, before reaching his hand over to her shoulder, holding around her with one arm, and giving her a slight but caring squeeze. Come on, time to make a move, let's see if we can get a bite to eat somewhere. As Flower was putting her socks back on, and adjusting her feet back into the padded skates, she had just one little request for the future. 'Will you help me with my English? I want to learn better, learn everything, to speak better, ok.' Facing her now, and with both of her hands in his, he helped her up to her feet, making sure she was steady enough not to fall over. 'Of course honey, and I'll make sure the others help you too, and thanks for asking about my family, it shows me how much you care.'

The bedroom, his room, their room, had been given up to me. He did this on the first night, and none of them ever complained since then, not once. I don't know if he has gotten used to sleeping in his chair, now that he has been sleeping in that same chair for so long. Or perhaps they just don't know any better, born into the chair, die in the chair, what else is there to know?

He gave me his room, and all his furniture to go with it, all he asked for was one drawer, that's it just a single drawer? The whole apartment was given up to me to use as my own, he made it feel like he was the guest, that he was the one that had intruded upon my life, inserting himself into my world, not the other way around. I have opened his drawer a few times, and nothing ever changes, he has the same clothes, everything he buys or wears is the same; the only colours he wears are white, grey and black, and occasionally a dark or navy blue. And everything is the same, his vests, his t-shirts, his hoodys, all white grey or black. And jeans, he wears jeans although I have only ever seen three pairs, so they seem to match the rest of his clothes. Doesn't he get bored? Doesn't he want some colour or variety in his life? I had thought about buying him some new clothes, but I was scared that he might not like them or perhaps would not even wear them. But what he does have is so cheap, I keep expecting to find holes in his clothes, perhaps he replaces them himself without me knowing? I do know one thing, he hates brands, all his vests and t-shirts are plain, no logo, no design, just blank. Even his hoodys don't have any writing or logos on them, perhaps just a small embroidered tag, nothing more, nothing noticeable.

It had been two months now, Flower had settled into the groove of answering the same questions about herself every day, and did so with ease and without frustration or anger. Some days were more exciting than others, but she didn't mind, she found herself devoting her entire day once he was awake to fulfilling all of his requests. They went bowling when he wanted to bowl, at times they ran out into the rain to play like two children, splashing around in the alleyway next to the apartment, sometimes they would endlessly walk the city, or just find a quiet corner, a hideaway to visit, and sit there in perfect happiness. It had been two months and still everyday she had to reassure him that correcting her English every time she made a mistake was a good thing, he always needed reassuring that he was helping, and not in fact being rude, some days it felt like she was starting all over again.

*

Waking up felt horrible, where the hell was I? Had we always slept like this? Was every morning a horrible awakening? I had woken up on an old blue leather chair, that creaked under every movement, I didn't feel as stiff as I thought I would, my feet were up on a foot rest, so I had slept in a semi-prone position, but as I stretched now and got up from the chair, I could feel that sleeping like this had not done my back any good. There was a note on the coffee table next to me, it was in my handwriting, so someone else who had lived in my body must have written it. It looked grubby and slightly tattered, but I thought that the first thing I should do is read it.

Flower had often wondered exactly what happened to him in the night, what was the transition like, when he believed that he died, and another one, another him was born, same body, same personality, no memory. Was it as simple as that, did he just have amnesia, a twenty four hour memory. But no that didn't feel right, Flower had seen him change from day to day, different attitudes, drives and interests. He could be lively and outgoing, then shy and retreating, both an extrovert and an introvert.

There were a few constants throughout; like the way he loved the park and nature, even in a more sombre mood, refusing to leave the apartment until Flower forced him out the door, either by threatening him or coaxing him. He had began to teach her English sayings as well, 'By hook or by crook' she always took him outside, to see the world, it would have been a sin to ever leave him indoors for a whole day, a whole lifetime, it would have been an opportunity lost.

He also never cooked, she did not know if he could or not, but they always went out to eat breakfast, sometimes they would buy sandwiches and eat them in the park, and dinner was always either a takeaway, or Flower would cook for them.

Sex was another constant, he never seemed to go out to bars to pick up women, nor had he ever made any advances towards her either. Apart from the first night they met, he had shown no interest whatsoever towards any carnal desires. Surely if he lived and died every day, if every meal was his first and last, then he would have also been a virgin over and over again, however this never seemed to bother him.

Flower felt that it was up to her to always energise him, to keep him moving, keep him busy. She did not know what had happened to him in the past, or for how long he had been like this, but she was going to make sure that while she was around, she would help him and would be there for him in every way she could. He had protected her, the first time they met, now it was up to her to nurture him, and his needs, for however long she could.

What was his driving force? What kept him going? Was it simpler to view life one day at a time, to make sure that you fully enjoyed every moment of it, Flower certainly felt like she was living her life to the fullest just by trailing in his wake. If he could live like this, why couldn't anybody? She had seen him wipe the slate clean, even after killing her captors, the deed was done, but now he has no memory or fault tying him to the what he did, he has managed to wipe the slate clean, the only problem was that he had wiped it too clean, every day was a new horizon, but had there been a incident in his past, a reason why he had made himself forget, Flower kept finding herself returning to the same dilemma, what had happened to him, why was he like this? What horrible reason was there for him to live like this? Did he really die every night? Had she found someone who was truly unique, one body that was shared by so many souls, he could have been a schizophrenic, but she did not believe that, not after looking into his eyes every day, and seeing the belief there and the burning passion to live. Was he one of Gods special children? A doorway for all those unborn souls, every unborn foetus, every still-born baby, to get one chance to see the daylight, even if they had to share, was it better than having never have existed at all, or did it just make it worse for them, to have glimpsed at everything that would not be theirs.

Having decided to stay up later than usual, Flower had now crept back into the living room once she knew he was asleep, she had never done this before, having respected his privacy as much as he respected hers. Curiosity had gotten the better of her, the desire to try to work out once and for all what he was really like. He had explained to her on a number of occasions that he had to be home before the end of the witching hour, sometimes he could delay the change, but never any later than one o'clock in the morning. He didn't have to be asleep when it happened, there was a strong memory from one of the others, before Flower had moved in to live with him, when he had deliberately stayed awake, either to force himself to gain another day through greed, or to test his own beliefs on his dying every day, he never said. The change had happened while he was awake, and it had left him feeling feverish and ill for hours, he had wretched violently, his body became wracked with a fever and he shook uncontrollably, his skin was cold and clammy, and his insides felt like they had simply dissolved away. This had not been the only time when he had been awake for the change, sometimes he just could not sleep, but he would in the end, his Soul would slip effortlessly away, to be replaced by the next one, never again had he ever tried to stay awake on purpose, that memory had haunted each and every one of them since then, like farm animals that know not to touch the electric fence, they might not have experienced the shock themselves, but others had, and the knowledge was there, ingrained in all of them.

He did not stir all night, there was no dramatic change that came over him, nor did his body go into fits and convulsions, he simply went to sleep and someone else woke up in his place.

The warmth within the stadium was a completely different contrast to the cold night air outside, neither of them had ever been to Madison Square garden before, and they did not know what to expect once they were inside. As they made their way to their seats, they could see the colourfulness of the crowd, many people were still arriving, carrying food, wearing their team colours, laughing and talking with excitement as they looked for their seats. Flower had never been to watch any sport live before, and so far the night did not disappoint, it was exciting just being there before the game, sitting in the stadium as it began to fill, surrounded by the hub of activity, and nothing had even happened yet. She was just drinking in the atmosphere, the hustle and bustle of the crowd, you could feel the electricity there, waiting to be released, Flower wondered if every sports event was like this. He had bought the tickets a few days ago, which was very strange and unusual as he never planned ahead, he never bought something or planned anything that he would not be directly involved with himself during that same day, he might buy beers or food for the version of himself that would come along tomorrow or the next day, but only after he himself had eaten and drank some of the same, least he miss out on something, some exciting flavour to be captured and savoured. So to buy basketball tickets was a massive turnaround in his normal routine behaviour, and not only that but Flower did not have to remind him either, he already knew when the day came. Flower did suspect that there was possibly a daily note left behind that reminded him about the tickets, or that the tickets themselves had been placed in a convenient place where they would be seen, but she never came across them in the kitchen or the bathroom, so this did leave her wondering if perhaps she was seeing a different side to him at last. Striking up the conversation, and hoping to stir a few emotions as well, Flower asked if he was a big fan of the New York Knicks, but he just answered that he did not support either team one way or another, he never supported any team or got excited at all during a game or while he was watching any sports, he just enjoyed watching the event without having to support one side or another, or one athlete more than his or her rival competitors. 'Why, who do you want to win?' Flower did not need long to answer that question at all. 'I want the other team to win, I want the Hornets to win.' It did not take too much prying to figure out why, Flower simply preferred the colour of the Hornets turquoise kit, the home team did not even get a look in, as their kit was white, and in Flowers eyes, nothing special to look at. As it happens it was a good night for Flower, her team won, and every time they scored she really got into the game, standing up and cheering along with everyone else. He remained seated the whole time, clapping both teams in acknowledgment of their efforts and their scoring prowess, although deep down he also wanted the Hornets to win, seeing how Flower had chosen them for herself, he could not side against her or support a rival team to hers.

During the half time interval Flower took advantage of the break in play to ask a few more of her own questions. Flower still had not grasped the fine art of conversation, she would jump into a conversation feet first and without tact, she would often broach subjects

41

that she probably shouldn't have, also her conversations often had no thread, they would end as abruptly as they had begun, only to continue a few hours later as if no time had passed in-between, he often thought that perhaps Flower was holding back during these intervals, taking her time to think on what she wanted to say next, or perhaps composing her English before she spoke out, but mostly it was just a reflexion on her scatty and erratic personality. 'So do you like basketball then? Is it your favourite sport?' Flower wanted to know if there was something special about this particular sport, why had he brought her here and not anywhere else, to have planned ahead, what was so special about tonight?

'No not really, I am not a great fan of American sports. I prefer football...' then turning to Flower to make sure that she understood. 'English football, proper football, I don't mean that American football, although I do enjoy watching that as well, I just did not want to confuse you about the two.' Then taking a second or two he just had to add '...and don't you dare call it soccer, I hate that name, it ain't soccer, it's football.' This should have given Flower the opportunity she needed to ask him about his past, but she was so excited about him opening up even in the slightest that she did not concentrate on his past, instead she focused all her questioning on sports; which ones he liked, what was his favourite sport, did he used to play sports etc. etc. if only she would have noticed the English inflections that he had used, she could have opened him up a bit more about his past and where he was from, but as it happens they just talked about American sports all night. 'I used to like all the American sports except baseball, I could not stand baseball, I thought it was dull, boring and pointless. I preferred American football, then basketball and then ice hockey, I never supported anyone or followed any particular team, they were just good sports to watch. I could not stand baseball though, that was until I actually sat down and watched a game, and what would you know, I started to get into it, then the more I watched the more I enjoyed it, and now I don't mind watching it, like all other sports, I could happily watch it anytime, I just wasn't giving it a chance before, everything deserves a chance, a bit like people, everyone deserves a chance, and sometimes people deserve a second chance too, that's what I gave baseball; a second chance.

The game ended with a win for our team, which made Flower happy, I had visions of her heckling the Knicks players as they walked off the court had they won, not a good idea when they are playing at home. Now that the game was over I was eager to get back to the flat, there would not be much time left for me by the time we got home, I felt tired and I was ready to crash out. Before leaving I decided to take flower and head into the store, maybe I could get her a little something, a memento of tonight. When we got to the store it was not too busy, most of the supporters must have done all of their shopping before the game, unfortunately all they sold there was the official merchandise of the home team, I should have known better, but I did not realise, I had expected to find some variety, perhaps just a few token keepsakes that represented the various teams of the NBA, well at least it was worth a look, and now we can leave for home. Leaving the store we made our way towards the nearest exits, most of the fans had left the Garden by now, however there were a few drunken fans milling around in the car park, I had just held the door open for Flower, I don't know who had taught me my manners, or where I got them from, I never had any cause to use them before. Before Flower came along, I never spoke to anybody, so I never needed to be nice or polite, but with her, she seemed to bring out the gentleman in me, not that she was a lady, but everybody deserves to be treated with respect. Did I used to treat strangers with respect, or was I just rude to them, I can't remember, I was trying to think back to the last time a waitress or store clerk served me, did I smile? Did I thank them, or just ignore them? I was just thinking about this while I was holding the door open for Flower, she stumbled slightly once she had gotten through the door, sometimes she liked to wear her trainers without tying up the laces, just letting her feet move around freely inside her shoes, I guess it was a fashion thing. However this often caused her to stumble or shuffle her feet as she trudged along. No sooner had I let the door swing from my hand than I heard a group of guys in the car park comment about this, they had seen Flower stumble forwards, almost drunkenly. 'Whoa, would you look at the state of that!' Cried out one of the group, in a loud whiney voice. All of his friends burst out laughing, and seeing me walk over to take Flowers arm another one of the group, thinking he was just as clever as his drunk and obnoxious friend added, 'Can you imagine taking that thing home with you? I mean, jeez what a mess, look at the state of her.' The whole group was in raptures of laughter, and looking up into my face Flower could see that I was not going to let this go, I could see the pleading in her eyes, 'They just drunk, they young. I have no time for them, let's just go.' But it was futile; she knew that I could not just let it be. Shaking my head, I looked down at her and replied 'No, I can't let them get away with that, I can't let anyone be

44

disrespectful towards you, you mean too much to me.'
Leaving Flower I walked straight over to the group of four lads, I had their attention now, but their cockiness had not subsided, they thought that they were safe as a group. Without saying a word I made a bee-line to the first one that decided to have a go at Flower, the loudest one of the group, he was a thin runt with short dark hair full of gel, like his friends he must have expected me to talk first, to demand and apology or to hurl abuse at them, so he just stood there taking a long drag on his cigarette, cocking his eyebrow as I approached, trying to display an air of nonchalance. I was not intimidated by the group, neither was I there to talk, they should have realised this, I struck him across the face with the back of my hand, bitch-slapping him, sending him and his smoke sprawling. Before his friends could react I grabbed the nearest one to me, good, it was the second one who had insulted Flower, I held him by the neck as I pummelled his face with my free hand, dropping him to his knees, but that did not stop me punching him, I hit him time and time again before I let him slide, groaning to the floor. Their two friends had run off, they had gasped in surprise as I struck their friend, and they had run off in horror as I beat their other friend mercilessly. I had wanted to hurt them as well, I wanted to hurt them for laughing, but no matter, I did not have long before the security guards would be rushing towards us, I would have just enough time to teach one little lesson. Walking over to the leader, the loud mouthed one of the group, I had not hit him hard, just enough to stun him, but there he was crawling on his belly, his baggy yellow basketball top was grimy from the wet asphalt of the car park, here was a fool who had never learnt how to be hit, his friend had taken a hell of a beating, but here he was acting the worse off

of the two. I quickly pinned him down, to late to try and get up to run now, he had his chance. With my knees on his shoulders, looking down on him, I just tut-ted, 'Tut-tut-tut, don't you know how to behave in front of a lady, you think you're a man, all cocky and full of bravado, try acting like a man, try being a gentleman instead, you see a girl fall down, help her up.' But he did not let me finish, he was whining and repeating how he will be more of a gentleman in future, saying I will, I will, I will over and over again. This just led me to shake my head even more, too late for that now, sometimes a lesson has to be harsh to be learnt. Looking around, I saw what I was after, ah yes, there it was, and just within reach too, grabbing his mouth to shut him up, I reached over for the stub of the cigarette, then brought it close to his face. 'You see, sometimes manners have to be learnt, and some lessons should not be forgotten, some actions should not be forgotten either, I'm going to make sure that you remember tonight for a long time, forever in fact. And leaning over him, I brought my hand down, searing the thin patch of skin below his eye, where his cheekbone was closest to the skin, I held it there a long time, through his screams I held it there, finally pushing it in deeper, knowing that it would leave a perfectly circular scar, a dot deep enough on his face to scar forever, leaving him with the mark of Cain. I left him there, clutching his face and sobbing, his friend gurgling and blowing red bubbles, with a broken nose and bent teeth. Flower had not moved during my retaliation, she just stood in the same spot calmly, as if she had seen it all before and worse, she took my arm, and resting her head against my shoulder we walked, leaving the lights of the car park behind us, we headed off into the dark city.

Lin

It was Friday night, and Flower had suggested that they go for a good old-fashioned steak, she had tried to discover what exactly counted as American cuisine, and apart from Meat Loaf, she was hard pressed to find anything that had originated here, so instead she decided to research the favoured eating habits of Americans instead. There wasn't much that she discovered she liked, preferring instead to eat Chinese or Korean food instead.

New York streets were a wonder in the nigh time, you could see the very best and very worst of the city. People moved in different circles, never leaving their comfort zones. Rich bankers along with shirt and tie office workers frequented the Irish pubs and the various bars where the staff served them with familiar faces, and they could blow off steam with cockiness and arrogance without drawing any unwanted attention or aggression from any other irritated drinkers. Who is going to feel grieved by a group of Wall Street hotheads who are engrossed in loud and leery drinking games, who climb up on top of stools and tables, and pinch the barmaid on the backside, before turning to their friends for a series of cheers and a round of back slapping. The whole bar was the same, and each bar was almost identical in it's atmosphere and it's company, arrogant and cocky drunks, each one a clone of the last, Rolexes and silk shirts, birds of a feather flock together, and in a city like New York, no one leaves their comfort zone.

They had decided to walk home after their meal down at the Steak House, too much meat had made them feel slow and sluggish and they were suffered the effects of having eaten too much. The night was warm and stuffy, but the slight breeze that picked up and then settled down in rare wisps brought some comfort from the summer evening heat.

My shirt has sticking to a patch on my back, where sweat had formed in a small oval, every time I peeled my shirt away, it just stuck back there again, blocking the pores and making me sweat even more. Flower did not look uncomfortable at all, she was used to hot and humid summers and freezing winters. I would have thought that she did not want to talk about China, but I was completely wrong, at every given opportunity she would compare how safe and friendly China was with how dangerous and dirty America was. But it wasn't just the main differences, everything was taken apart and criticized by her, the food was better, the girls prettier, the streets safer, you could haggle in the shops, there was a great depth of history and culture. And as it happens it was exactly that that we were talking about that evening while we were walking home. 'The problem with America, it has no culture. Everyone is spoilt and selfish, want, wan't, want, me, me, me. I won't raise my children here, they will grow up to be brats. And the worse thing is, there is plenty of culture and history here, but the Americans destroy it all, American Indian culture is so beautiful, but no one here care. They want to start their history from now, so they make war. Start again with white history, try to wipe out Red Indian history, maybe after long enough they will not exist anymore, and maybe then the rest of the world will forget them. Americans are invaders here anyway, this is not their country, they really Europeans...'

I had carried on walking, not noticing that Flower had stopped talking, I was not sure if she wanted me to reply or to put in any input of my own? I had decided to let her rant on undisturbed, once she got into the swing of things. I'm sure that that is what the others do anyway, so she probably would not mind or even notice me doing the same. It was then that I noticed that she was no longer walking beside me, turning around I could see her crouching down next to a homeless person. Sighing deeply I walked quickly back to go and get her.

As I neared I could see that the homeless figure that was sitting on an old church wall was in fact a woman. I could not make out what Flower was saying to her, as she was speaking in Mandarin, and doing so very quickly. As soon as I began listening to what Flower was saying, she suddenly stopped talking. Turning to me she said 'She is not Chinese, Vietnamese I think, or maybe somewhere around there, Laos, Cambodia, who knows? She can not speak English. We should take her home, give her somewhere to live, something to eat, ok.' This did not sound like a request, and what did I care anyway, I would be gone soon.

I don't know which movement the girl understood, if it was Flower miming putting food into her mouth and rubbing her belly, doing an unconvincing mmm, or the wild actions that incorporated her story that involved walking, following, eating sleeping and for some reason getting dressed. The getting dressed part did confuse me, did Flower mean getting dressed after a bath or buying new clothes? It did not matter anyway, the Vietnamese girl seemed to be following, reluctantly walking five steps behind us, but following all the same, she did keep looking over her shoulders, but did not mutter another word the rest of the journey home.

In the flat I left the girls too it, I did not want to interfere or be underfoot in any way, I also thought that two strange foreigners speaking rapidly in English and Mandarin would not put the poor girl at ease, and watching Flower open and close the front door three times over to hopefully demonstrate that it was not locked and that she could leave at any time did seem comical, but I was trying not to laugh. I'd let her settle down and feel a bit more comfortable before I would go over and say anything to her, so Instead I sat down and made myself comfortable and began to write.

The rules might not have been in a constant state of flux, but they had been added to, that much was clear, and not by Flower herself, but by one of us, the handwriting was definitely ours, there was no mistaking that, although the new rules appeared cramped and scrambled as they had been squeezed onto the same page, some were written above or below the original rules, some were along the side of the page, and some were in the margin. The page now looked like a timeline, how the rules had evolved to cater for the unforeseen rescue of a certain Chinese girl, and now they had to evolve further. The first rules had been basic, written out of fear from the one who saved her, a fear that he did not know what the next one to follow him would do, so he had irrationally tried to control the situation and the path that all our lives would take, the feeling of helplessness that he must have felt, what was it like? I felt really close to him now, to Flowers saviour, I find myself in the same situation, whatever I write tonight will pave the future for both girls, Flower and the stray homeless Vietnamese girl who has followed us home. Of course she might not be here when the morning comes around, in fact they might have both left by then, but Flower is her own person, she can come and go as she pleases, and as long as she is here I'll look after her, as far as the Vietnamese girl go's, well I'll find out her story soon enough. There was still enough room on the page for me to add what I needed to add, I wrote in-between the current rules that were noted down, I added references to the new girl, squeezing them in where I could, but at the same time I tried not to take up too much space, I could not fill the page, I needed to leave room, some room for any future unforeseen eventuality, who knows how the rules will evolve further from this point onwards?

*

Days had passed and it was evident that all three occupants of the apartment had fallen into a routine. There were no arguments, no misunderstandings, everyone just lived together doing their own thing, it felt like all the inhabitants of the apartment were sharing it with two other ghosts, nothing happened, but no one got under anyone else's feet either, things lasted like this for a while, a constant calm and serine routine. The Vietnamese girl slowly became accustomed to life in the apartment, and nothing was strange or new to her anymore.

Flower continued to mother Lin, making sure she ate, and was generally comfortable in all respects. The girl was quiet and shy, and seemed to resign to her fate, allowing Flower to think for her in every aspect of her life. She was just happy to be underneath someone else's wing I suppose.

51

At least we were glad that Flower had sense enough not to buy her clothes that were not the same style as her own, one walking fashion statement was enough, but two would just give us a headache, instead she let Lin choose the shops she wanted to shop in, letting her select the clothes that she was comfortable in. How long would this pattern of co-existing life last for? Was it comfortable for us living like this, was it comfortable for all three of us? Had we ever suffered from paranoia before? Had we ever wondered or suspected that the two of them would be plotting against us, planning to kick us out of the flat, away from our nest, our refuge? They could have the whole place to themselves, and what would we do then? Where would we go? Would the next one of me wake up never remembering the mutiny, thinking that we had always lived on the street? Perhaps one day walking past them in the street, oblivious of the betrayal, not realising that the whole time they would be sniggering as they saw how low we had fallen.

*

Morning routines had become quite different, the day would start with a brief lesson in Mandarin, so before Flower would wake, I had gotten into the routine of waking early, early enough to look over my notes before Flower woke up. I was still struggling with the writing, but at least I could communicate at the basest level, and my lack of an American accent was helping me to get the correct pronunciation, although I still could not get to terms with the idea that changing the pitch of a word ended up altering its meaning.
The kitchen had developed a rash of yellow post-it notes, it had taken days, but the hard work was worth it,

and it was not just the kitchen either, the whole apartment had been transformed, every surface, every item now had its own description in Vietnamese, Mandarin and English written on each little yellow note. Everything had it's label, everything from the kettle and the toaster to the food in the fridge. This was done in order for Lin to live more comfortably here, it also helped her a lot with learning English, and it seemed to be paying off, slowly but surely we were communicating together, life was getting easier in the flat, the Vietnamese and the Mandarin was also helping me learn, although I preferred writing the mandarin using the English alphabet, in order for me to learn the correct pronunciation, so I wrote them all phonetically, which annoyed Flower because she thought I was shrugging my responsibility with regards to learning the Chinese characters, but at least I was learning Mandarin, and learning it my way.

I don't know how accurate the Vietnamese dictionary was, but Lin seemed to be pleased, she had had to amend a few of the notes, but she understood and appreciated the effort that Flower and I had gone to. So Lin was learning English, I was learning Mandarin and Vietnamese and Flower was content to teach Lin and myself, without learning any new language herself.

*

My Vietnamese was still at the basic level of greeting, meaning that I could say hello; good morning, yes, no, thank you, your welcome, food, drink, excuse me, goodnight. I was secretly hoping that Lin would learn English faster than I could get to grips with Vietnamese. I had begun to learn Mandarin out of interest one day while I was bored, but after struggling

53

so much and seeing so little progress I began to feel dejected, and to be honest my heart was not in learning two new languages side by side, it was irritating and confusing.

*

So there we had it, Flower had come up with a plan, one that might give a new lease of life to all three of us. I did not know whether or not it would work, but that would remain to be seen, I was willing to go along with it, I mean why not, it was an interesting concept after all.

The first thing that needed to be done was to replace Lin's passport, I had thought of going down to Chinatown and beating someone for the sake of their passport, but as Flower then pointed out, for her to be able to pass as a Chinese she would need to speak Chinese. So from somewhere we would need to get a Vietnamese passport, or more accurately I would have to get one for her.

*

As it turned out Lin had suffered greatly, losing out to bad luck, the end result had left her sheltering outside the old church, homeless, hungry and in despair, she was still at the same church two weeks later when we found her. Saigon was her home, the maps might call her home city Ho Chi Minh city, as a tribute when the American war had ended, but all the inhabitants still called it Saigon. A year previously she had met an American English language teacher living in Saigon, he was young and kind and had a fair grasp of Vietnamese, and unlike all the other foreigners he was a rare find, he

54

was a western male in Asia who did not just use the local girls for sex.

His job paid well, and he had been supplied with a furnished apartment rent free under his contract with the school, although she did not move in with him, she did see him there every day. Their love blossomed and Lin could not come to terms with what would happen when he would have to leave to return home, she tried not to think of it, until it was too late, the reality of his visa expiring and his time in Vietnam was coming to an end was all too real. He had never spoken about wanting to show his home to Lin, neither had he ever spoken much about America as a whole, unbeknownst to Lin he had always hoped to get his visa extended for another year, but his re-application had been refused .

Lin had cried as she held him, her tears had run down her face soaking a patch on his t-shirt, saying her goodbyes in the airport had seemed like a blur. She felt too ill to talk when they had sat down for a coffee, and she would not let go of his hand the whole time that they had walked around the airport together, and now she was saying goodbye, she just held him as tightly as she could. She would not have called it a goodbye hug, she was just holding him, as she felt her heart breaking, she would not let go, he would have to be the first to break away, if he was leaving her for ever then he would have to break their embrace as well. He said that it was time now for him to go, he had to go, he said he was sorry, he told her he loved her. His blonde wavy hair and beautiful face was a pink blur now, Lin's eyes were blurry with tears, and wiping them had not helped her to see clearly, he kissed her again even though her lips were quivering, and he walked away, Lin could still not see him clearly, she gave a sob, was he crying too, she could not tell, she wiped her eyes again and tried to wipe her wet cheeks, was he crying? She could not see, she sobbed louder, he was through the gate now, she could still make out his orange rucksack, his carry-on luggage was like a beacon in the crowd, it reminded her of an orange buoy out in a storm, only appearing every now and again in-between the waves to show that it was still there, and that it had not been swallowed up and lost.

*

It had been a quiet rainy day, spent walking around the city, in and out of shops for shelter, even though no one had even bought anything, it was just nice to get out of the never ending drizzle. The only highlight had been Brooklyn bridge, although I did not see the point. It was a famous landmark for some reason, and I had taken the girls there, but one big blustery bridge was the same as any other in this city, I was not even sure if I had the right bridge. But it hardly mattered, the noise of the traffic was unappealing and there was no view through the mist, so sodden and miserable we walked in the direction of home.

After only fifteen minutes of walking Flower came up with a novel idea, we had just passed a Vietnamese restaurant when Flower called us back, and suggested that we had dinner there, I did not care either way, the day had been dull and disappointing all round, so the thought of cooking when I was wet and miserable was unappealing. The entrance was crowded with three young Vietnamese girls, all wearing a long sleek black dress with gold trim, standing next to a tall wooden pedestal that contained the nights list of bookings, the concierge greeted us without even smiling, talking to us long enough to ask how many of us needed to be seated, before leaving us to the waitress that was standing next to her; who then lead us to a table at the far end of the restaurant, next to an enormous fish tank, the waitress was decent enough to smile, which instantly washed away the grudge that I could feel building up towards the concierge, how did I know what kind of day she had had before now, so pushing first impressions aside, we all sat down, and I began to feel less tense. A jug of water was brought over along with the menus, then the waitress returned with more servicttcs after she noticed that we had already used ours up to dry our faces and hands. I had never thought of buying an umbrella before, much preferring to sully my depressive moods in the rain. But looking at the two sorry excuses for women who were sitting together across the table from me, Flower looked like the epitome of misery, while Lin looked like a river had washed her away. Flowers hair was a tangled mess, and her face was smudged where the constant drizzle had soaked her make-up and whilst she had tried to dry her face, she had applied too much pressure around the eyes, causing them to seem darker towards the corners, I often thought that she did this on purpose, preferring the dishevelled and ungraceful look to her appearance.

*

Alone in her room, Flower had stripped to near nakedness, she was just standing next to the window in her underwear, her right shoulder resting against the wall, as she leaned her bodyweight against it, her left finger tracing raindrops, from the inside of the window as they fell down. A few moments passed and then she returned to her wooden chair next to the small desk in her room. She did not know what the desk had been used for before, but since she had moved into the apartment, she had introduced many items to it that would aid her with her sewing, this included a large mirror that squared off directly in front of her, and a smaller circular mirror with lights around it, like an upside down circular dentist light, just with a mirror in the middle. Flower removed her bra, set it down on the desk, reached over to her sewing kit, thought better of it, reached for another bra to put on, then returned to her sewing kit. Flower had collected a vast array of delicate accessories from shops and department stores all over the city, she browsed in them almost daily, least she miss out on buying a hidden treasure that she might never come across again. She had just the right idea for the dark blue bra in her hand, all along the top ridge of the cup, on both sides she would sew on little daises, she was not sure if they were meant to be buttons or not, but she thought that three either side would prove to be ideal, and so with her light fingers and thread she set to work. After only attaching the second daisy, Flower suddenly realised that she had lost all track of time, and she got up and rushed to the bedroom window. It was still raining outside, but the rain was falling more lightly now, the sound of traffic could be heard on the wet streets below her. Ten minutes had passed before she saw him, and there he was, jogging across the street, wearing the same long brown coat without a hood, and today he had no hat on either, so as he stepped into the shelter of the doorway of the cafe where he worked, he paused to brush his hands against his crew-cut sending a light spray of water upwards like a mist. Flower traced one of her fingers against the cold, condensed window, in the repeated pattern of a small circle, then about five seconds after he had gone inside the cafe, she eased her wet finger under the cup of her bra, placing it directly on her nipple, sending a chill down her spine, and she groaned lightly. A few seconds passed as she stood there, she sucked her lower lip inside her mouth, before slowly releasing it, letting it roll back, her two front teeth applying more pressure downwards on the lip itself as she did so, not hard enough to be uncomfortable, but with enough pressure to invoke her sensual urges, then releasing herself from her fantasy, Flower returned to her desk and her embroidery.

All in all Flower had designed, re-designed, altered, and transformed eighteen bras and four pairs of underwear. It had taken her four different trips to Macy's before she bought her first pack of little embroidery patches, they were meant for a little girl to have on her school bag, but Flower had decided that they looked too nice not to buy, she had never used some of them, but a rainbow was perfect for her, and on second thoughts she had also sewn on the pink unicorn on the opposite cup, the shooting star she had kept for another day, instead attaching it above the rainbow, when she was depressed and needed something to cheer her up Flower always turned to her creative designs and her sewing. Since that first bra she had worked in many different mediums, preferring to keep her original inspiration as it was, she never sought to add to it with any further patches. Some bra's were garish and outlandish, three were completely covered, patches were even laid on top of patches, and not a single patch of the original material was showing. They were mindboggling collages, but Flower would have derived a lot of pleasure from having the man she lusted after staring at them for hours on end, taking time to search out the different patterns and pictures, appreciating the hours of effort and preparation that was put into each one.

Flower's designs ran in timelines of certain genres, where she would design a few bra's in certain styles, before moving on to a different style, the only unusual thing about it would be that once she had decided to move on to another certain type of design, she would then never return to that style again. Perhaps her most original idea had been when she designed her own flag motif on her bra's, it had began with a red bra with a large gold star on the outside and four smaller identical stars below it and to the right. Following this Flower also created a Scottish and Swedish flag design, and two Jamaican designs, one where there was a separate flag for each cup and the other where the cross design of the bra itself stood for the yellow saltier cross with black cups on either side and green straps and trim. Her current inspiration was communism, Flower was not political in anyway, no more than anyone else she knew, she supported the Peoples Party, but then again she would have supported whoever was in power, politics for her was something that happened far away and existed in only the distant past and the far future. She had a black bra with a red star, a red bra with a golden sickle and hammer, and now she was working on an olive green bra with a large red star on the left side, too big for the cup itself, some of the star's points had been cut off.

To begin with Flower would find herself waiting by the window as often as three or four times a week, but now she knew the work rota of the young man she admired, she was able to gage what time to wait and look out for him to within ten minutes of his arrival at work in the cafe. She never told the others of her love interest across the street, neither did she ever recommend going to the cafe at any time. He had been there many times, and most of the time Flower and Lin would go too, but

60

never by themselves, they never went anywhere by themselves, feeling vulnerable without his company, his safety. The cafe however remained the only place where he would ever find himself alone, what did he think about while he was there? He certainly never had a moment alone in the apartment, and they always went together everywhere else, without exception, so what could happened to him over breakfast, while he was alone with his thoughts, their thoughts, their many thoughts?

*

We were becoming increasingly worried about Lin, I believe it is her nature to be quiet and shy, but as time has been passing, she does not seem to be engaging herself in any way, neither is she coming out of her shell. It is true she does accompany Flower and us when we go out on our excursions, either to the shops, a restaurant or the park, for example, but not once has she ever recommended something for us to do, or shown the slightest interest in anything for herself. Flower has been dragging her along to the cinema in order to see as many English films as she can, hoping that it would improve her English, but not once has she ever asked to go out anywhere, so finally we decided to take her to a bookshop. We don't know where the idea came from, and neither was it planned, the three of us were walking through the city one day, when suddenly we saw a bookshop across the street, and we came up with an idea, we told Flower and Lin that we must go there and once the traffic had stopped the three of us crossed, we trail blazed the way forwards, Lin and Flower following in our wake. We took Lin by the hand and dragged her up to the second floor, ah there it was the Hobbies section, gardening, arts and crafts, D.I.Y. flower arranging all that we needed to know to find out about what Lin's interests were, she could just point at what she wanted to do or indeed liked to do, and then we would buy the book for her and pursue her interests.

As it happens Lin did not have any hobbies, she did not do any sports, she did not collect anything, or make anything, but our mad dash to the book shop was not in vain, as we were standing a bit dejected, Flower had wondered off following a young, tall shop clerk and was currently telling him how cute she thought the bookmarks were, the only problem was that instead of leaning on to the counter where the bookmarks were, she had invariably dived onto the counter to reach the furthest ones, so her feet were dangling a few inches off the ground, her toes tapping against the counter wall in an alternative thudding motion, showing her childlike crush. However lying half on top of the counter did nothing to hide her childishness or her dignity, as her underwear was showing to the disgust of the queue behind her, not only had she pushed ahead of everyone to continue talking to the clerk as he walked behind the counter to put down the bundle of books in his arms, but she was also showing the world her turquoise thong, whether they wanted to see it or not. As we turned away from Flower, the disgruntled shoppers behind her, and the embarrassed clerk, Lin suddenly grabbed us by the sleeve and tugged us, rushing off to the Art section, as it happens, she had no interest at all in painting or sketching, but she had a great love for art, and after we purchased a few art books for her, she would often sit gazing at the pages for hours. As time went by, we could offer her better than this, and we would often frequent the great art galleries of this city, Lin sitting in silence, staring at the paintings with a grin on her face, as we often found ourselves frowning at Flower's lack of ability to act ladylike in the calm and quiet oasis of the gallery.

It had taken a lot longer than he had expected, but finally the parcel had come, it had to be pried out of Flowers hands, but he did not want her to open it, not yet, he had to inspect the contents first. He did not blame her for protesting loudly as she sat down at the kitchen table, ready to open it, after all it had been addressed to her, but he had to address it to her, he could not put his name down, so instead he addressed it to Flower, the parcel did need something more than just an address on it after all, he could have put Lin's name down, but that would not have been fair, there was nothing for Lin inside the box, and he could not disappoint her like that, it would be cruel to let her think that there was something special for her, only to give it to Flower once it was unwrapped.

He had hoped to answer the door first, hoping to take the parcel from the postman himself, but Flower had beaten him to it while he was brushing his teeth. So Flower had been told to wait, he could hear her heavy handed footsteps from the bedroom, she was stomping around on purpose out there, trying to make as much noise as she could, letting him know how irritated she was. This made him laugh, let her bang against the furniture, it is a gift for her after all, soon she will be jumping up and down with joy, and wrapping her arms around his neck, she always did this, but sometimes as she did she would bend both knees simultaneously, hanging from him like a child, so he would have to remember to be prepared or else they would both fall into a heap on the floor. Pulling out the invoice and putting it in his pocket, he then turned to the turquoise blue basketball shirt, ah yes, perfect, no holes no tears, perfect condition, he hoped that Flower would like it, she had enjoyed the game that she had been taken to, and the three of them often went to the local sports bar to watch any other Hornets games that were being shown on television. Underneath the shirt were two key rings, depicting the Blue and purple Hornet mascot, a cartoon figure with a basketball in one hand, and trainers on its feet. That would do nicely, one for him and one for Flower, to put on their keys to the flat. He had not forgotten about Lin, he could not give something to Flower and not to her, or the other way around either. He had bought Lin a small dark red Buddha statue that he had found in the Chelsea markets, and to go with it a beautiful circular jade pendant, the jade was polished with a hole in the middle, he did not know if the Vietnamese were fond of Jade, or even if Lin would like the gifts, but he hoped so. He had been dying to give them to her for a long time, but he needed the parcel to arrive first, or it would not be fair, and he had been waiting for this parcel for an even longer time. When he came out of the bedroom Flower was indeed overjoyed, he did not know if she would actually wear the basketball jersey, but she wanted to try it on straight away, even getting changed in the kitchen. As always modesty was lost with her.

*

My memory was improving, Flower had noticed this too, she said it had not taken long, only a week or two after she had moved into the apartment after the night where We had saved her, she said that to begin with I would wake and would have to read the note every time, every day. Not knowing what had happened before, but then gradually we no longer needed to read the note, we knew what had happened, what had occurred before. Before we used to wake up to a new world, new experiences, to be savoured and cherished, our past wiped away, the base knowledge was still there, we knew our way around the city, we knew where we liked to eat, we remembered everything we had learnt previously and we knew where our money was hidden and how much was left, but every day was like the first day, but now not any more. We still woke up, being born into this world; then when we slept at night we would die, it was a simple enough life, and one that would have gone on undisturbed, had it not been for Flower and Lin.

*

We had walked to central park, stopping at a small bakery to buy stale bread in order to feed the ducks. Flower was in her curious mood as the both of us stood throwing little pieces of bread and crust into the water, Lin was sitting beneath a nearby tree, watching butterflies flitter past. 'So, you die every night, but how? I mean...do you have to be asleep to die? What if you are awake all night? Will you live? Maybe you can stay awake, two three days, then the curse can be broken.' I tried telling her that it was not a curse, it was just our way of life. 'But don't you want to live, live forever, live normally?' She replied.

She was throwing large chunks of stale French bread into the pond now, I could tell that she was frustrated, and she wanted to help us, to understand us better. Her splashes were scarring the ducks away, but I did not say anything, she would only turn around and tell me off for not taking her seriously. 'Ok tonight, we stay awake, you and me, all night, no sleeping, Lin can stay up to, or go to sleep, up to her, but I won't, I will watch you, and you will watch me, no sleeping ok. But this would not make any difference, the change would still come over me, it just would not be as comfortable as going to sleep and letting the next one wake up to a new life, it would be like wrenching him into life with a shock, he would find himself suddenly and abruptly alive with no warning, and I worried that this might affect our memory, what if he reverted back to our former lack of long term memory, what if we never regained the capacity for memory that we had now fought so hard to gain. What if the shock caused him to act violently, no the risk would be too great with the girls around. We had done it before, I am sure of it, but with no one else around, being in a psychotic state alone in a flat does not harm anyone, only the furniture. Flower then suggested that maybe we change because we are in our comfort-zone, I was impressed with her choice of words, her English had improved a lot lately. She said that being in our chair, in our apartment was too convenient, too comfortable, she said that we were letting the change happen, we should be out in the city, not in anywhere public, like a bar, but just walking the streets all night, to see what would happen. She seemed to think that what occurred to us might happen like clockwork, that at the stroke of midnight, one of us would replace the other, I tried explaining that it was not as simple or as precise as that, the change did indeed occur sometime after midnight, but what time I am not sure, sometime between midnight and one o'clock in the morning; the end of the witching hour. This in fact stirred a memory in me, of waking up alone in the dark in our apartment, it was past eleven o'clock, and the change had not occurred yet, one of us had gone to sleep, only to wake before his death, alone, cold and scared in the world, with only a few minutes to himself, extra time that had been gained, time where he was alive but did not want to be, thinking of that cold sweat sent shivers down my spine, and left me feeling empty and frightened, I never wanted to feel like that again. I told her it would not make any difference, we could be walking along, but when the time came I would just stop for an instant, as if remembering something would break my stride, a moment or two would pass where I would stand there with my eyes closed, perhaps there would be a look of concentration on my face, but once my eyes would open, they would no longer be my eyes, they would be the next one's and he would probably be wondering why he was outside in the cold and the dark instead of being in our apartment, of course I did not mention the violent convulsions, the fever or the severe nausea that would invariably follow for several hours afterwards, I did not want to distress Flower. After hearing my limited and poor explanation Flower became even more frustrated, she threw the rest of the bread into the pond in one go, and stormed off. I did not mean to upset her, I was glad that she cared for me, I loved her so much, I had never loved anything before, or not as far back as we could remember anyway. I looked over to Lin, who had fallen asleep underneath the shade of the tree, I cared for her too, how had it come to this, to love and care for two people, to have their lives thrust into mine, for me, for us to be such an integral part of their lives, for them to become so dependent on me, on all of us?

*

It had been raining heavily, and after lunch they had returned to the flat, he doubted that they would be going out again, and seeing how Lin was in the bathroom and Flower was using the hairdryer he made the most of the opportunity to go into the bedroom to get a dry change of clothes, when he opened his drawer he was surprised to find the blue Hornets basketball jersey folded nicely on top of his clothes. Did this mean that Flower did not like her gift? Did she no longer wish to wear it? It had not been there this morning when he went to get changed, so flower must have slipped it in before they went out. Then he realised that Flower had been wearing her basketball jersey today, he noticed it before she put her coat on, this meant that she had gone to the effort of buying him this jersey. Lifting it out of the drawer he could see that yes indeed it was a different jersey, it was a larger size and slightly worn, with a different pattern on the trim, perhaps Flower had been to a second hand shop to buy it for him, or maybe she saw it in a market while they were out. Smiling he put it on, then changed from his wet jeans, and selecting a dry hoody he went back to the living room, a little colour would not be too bad, the colour suited Flower, and it kind of looked good on him too, smiling to himself as he closed the bedroom door behind him, he was glad of the gift.

*

The alarm went off, ringing in my ear, and I quickly reached for it and switched it off before it woke anyone up. I knew what to do, I remembered, but just in case there was a note on my chest, I sat up in the chair, went over to open the fridge in order to read the note without having to turn any lights on. It was time, the alarm had woken me up at two o'clock in the morning, I knew what I needed to do, I grabbed my bag, it was already packed with one clean change of clothes and a spare pair of trainers. I grabbed my knuckle dusters, a flick knife and my wallet and went out the door, I had an appointment to keep.

*

Flower was in the bathroom, and had been for a long time now, she always took such a long time in there, Lin had long silky black hair, so I understood the fact that it took her a long time to wash, clean and dry her hair, but Flowers hair was quite short and frizzy, and she had been doing something to her fringe lately that cave it a crinkled look, like the crinkle cut chips from back home. Her normal long sessions in the bathroom had now taken on a whole new lease of life, they had been extended up to mammoth proportions.

Flower was never shy around Lin and myself, and we were used to seeing her parade around the flat in her underwear, either to show off her new home made designs, or because sometimes she thought that wearing your underwear actually counted as getting dressed. In the mornings before breakfast she would often visit the kitchen to get a glass of juice wearing only her knickers, her breasts exposed and her nipples standing out after receiving a blast of cold air from the fridge, she would then return for breakfast, believing herself to be adequately dressed by only having slipped on either a bra or a T-shirt, and still not covering herself up properly with shorts or jeans. Lin was a different matter, she never left the bedroom undressed, and no matter the weather or what time of day it was, she never took off the same green jacket that she always wore. I

69

think her boyfriend gave it to her when he was still in Vietnam, either that or he left it behind, lost or forgotten while he was packing to leave. It was one of those fashionable army jackets, not a real army jacket of course, but one that designer clothes shops sometimes liked to sell, with two stripes on the right sleeve, quite like a sergeant's stripes, but with one less yellow bar. I was not schooled in army ranks, but this could quite possibly be a corporal's insignia. On the front were three small patches, one was the profile of a white eagles head, there was one gold star above the front pocket, and the third was a shield split in two colours, white and blue with a laurel wreath reaching up behind it, showing it's leaves either side. The inside of the jacket was a type of fleece material that was very soft and warm, which added to his memory when she wore it I am sure. She did keep it clean though, washing it at night when it needed cleaning, but to be fair to her, she did wear it every day, even if it was far too big for her, causing her to roll up the sleeves quite a few times until her fingers were visible.

So the three of us had come to an understanding, to have to wait for flower to leave the bathroom was impossible once she was in there, you either had to rush in there first if you really needed to go, or once she was in there resign yourself to only brushing your teeth or having a wash. Lin did not seem to mind, Flower would talk to her while she was in the bath, or shaving her legs, and Lin would smile and chat as she got herself ready for bed, I think they enjoyed it, neither of them had any sisters, and being close enough with someone to always feel comfortable in their presence showed how much the two of them had bonded together.

So into the bathroom I went, never knowing quite what to expect, and there I found Flower, soaking in the bath, like the queen of Sheba. She had been in there for over an hour, so I don't know if she had been busying herself first before she ran the bath, or if she had been continually topping it up in order to stay warm and not to get a chill. I had come in to shave as it was eight o'clock and I did not fancy having to shave any later than this, I had planned on making a cup of tea and eating a single slice of Victoria sponge cake which I had been looking forward to since my first slice at lunchtime. I had not come into this world with any stubble, I awoke clean shaven, and I planned on leaving our body the same way that I had found it for the next one and his arrival tomorrow. And if I did not shave now, then leaving it for later on would put me in a foul mood, a mood that I did not want to be in, my whole day was prepared in my head, hour by hour, and the remaining few hours were put aside for relaxing, to sit comfortably in my chair, with a cup of hot tea and a slice of cake, I was going to glide through a book on the Impressionists that Lin had lent me, and perhaps listen to classical music on the kitchen radio depending on how my mood was. When I walked in Flower was laying on her back, reading a book about a Chinese empress, either that or a royal concubine, Flower had mentioned the book before, but it did not peak my interest enough to listen to what the character's history was, neither was I sure whether it was fiction or not. Flower was engrossed in the book, and I was proud to notice that she had kept the pages dry, the corners had not even curled up due to neglect or mistreatment either, which was a real shock considering how she liked to just drop her possession wherever she pleased, Flowers wardrobe was a heap on the floor, while she took care of her hand made underwear by storing them in a drawer, she had given up every other drawer to Lin, who's sole wardrobe consisted of only a meagre collection of small flowery blouses, jeans and t-shirts.

The rest of the bathroom had taken on a life of itself, and things had sprung up all around as if a great ceremony was taking place around the central alter, which just happened to be the bath. There were little candles everywhere, giving off their little flicker towards the door as I came in. Flower's wine glass was still half full, although the bottle of rose was now empty. On the corner of the bath was a small plate, which I suspected had once held her beef and lettuce sandwich which I saw her making earlier, and dotted along the edge of the bath next to the wall were three fairy cakes, standing to attention like soldiers between two equally small fairy light candles. Well she had really gone full out this time, it looked like she was here for the duration, I just hoped that she was not going to fall asleep in the bath, I would have to remember to send Lin in here to check up on her later, to make sure she was still awake, once I had finished shaving of course.

The steam in the bathroom made the air to hot and too dry for me to bear so I left the door open, I could have opened the window as well, but I did not want Flower to get a chill so I left it closed. She had begun her event of an evening by having a bubble bath, although only a few solitary clumps of bubbles remained, clinging on to the islands that were her knees, and the rim of the bath in places, in the vain hope that they would not perish. The mirror was sodden, and wiping it with a towel just smeared the moisture across it, it was far too wet in here to dry the mirror properly, so I just carried on applying my shaving cream, watching the blurred image in the mirror intently, and using my fingers as a guide on my face to search for patches of stubble. Flower's wine glass made a soft clink on the corner of the bath as she replaced it, and knowing that she was too comfortable to leave her bath just yet, I fetched her glass and went to the kitchen to open another bottle of wine, pouring her half a glass before returning to wash my face. My eyes were quite tired now, maybe from the long day, or from the heat of the bathroom, it was nice and refreshing to splash cold water on them, it made me feel almost alive again as I repeatedly drenched my face with the icy cold water, a second time, then a third. I heard splashing behind me, and I turned around to see that Flower had turned over to lie on her front. She was still reading her book in this peculiar fashion, I could not fathom how this position could be comfortable in any way, wasn't her back uncomfortable like this? Didn't she have to cram her head back in order to read and keep her book dry, this could not have been comfortable for her neck surely, and what about her legs, with the bath too small her knees were now constantly bent and in just a few seconds her feet would get cold, and remain that way until she deemed ready to change her position again.

I had been staring at her for quite a while without noticing, just subconsciously looking at her in amazement as I dried my face and my neck over and over again, half expecting her to change position again right in front of me, waiting for her neck, her back or her knees to realise that she had made a bad judgement and she should resume her reading while lying on her back or by sitting upright again. But she was quite content, she just continued reading, and regardless of what it looked like to me, she seemed quite comfortable. I knew I was looking at her, and had been

73

for a while, but I had not noticed quite how much I was staring at her now, her buttocks were raised above the waterline, not like the archipelago of her knees as before, but like a mound rising up out of the deep, an Atlantis that had risen. Of all the times that I had seen her naked and in near states of nakedness and semi nakedness I had never looked at her lustfully before, I knew she was attractive, but I never saw her that way myself, none of us did. But now, she looked quite different, like a temple goddess, lying there surrounded by candles and offerings, waiting and wanting to be worshiped. I could feel the heat of the bathroom get to me, I could feel my head swimming as a rush of endorphins and adrenaline flooded my system, my heart missed it's beat and something rose up to catch in my throat, as if my throat was closing in on itself, getting narrower and narrower and constricting itself, restricting the flow of oxygen. I stumbled a few steps towards the bath, giddy like a school boy who has a crush on his teacher, silent and embarrassed. I knelt down beside the bath, she was so beautiful lying there, her skin had a golden hue to it as it glowed with the light of the candles and the mist of the room. Her skin glistened as the light shone off it, I could tell that the lotion from the bubble bath and the shampoos in the water had left her skin with a waxy and greasy sheen. I could not help myself, I could not resist, and I don't know why, I felt myself drawn to her perfect ripe bum as it rested there right in front of me. I reached out to touch her buttocks with my right hand, caressing the furthest cheek with my hand, gently and slowly I grasped it three times, each time letting the tips of my fingers dip into the bath water, to feel the drips release themselves once they had let go of her buttock, just to wash down into the water again. Although Flower was

74

more than just surprised by this, she was not startled. She did not flinch away or roll around thrashing in the water, she just looked up from her book, quite surprised, looking straight ahead at the taps, waiting to see what I would do next. But this was not a sexual impulse, I was not driven by lust or longing to be with her or with anyone. I was not after sex, otherwise I would have slid my arm around her waist, dipping my sleeve into the water, pulling her body close to mine, ready to kiss her and pull her from the tub into my arms. Neither was this an act of love, I loved Flower and Lin both, but I was not in love with either of them, nor did I or any of the others harbour any romantic thoughts or fantasies towards them, if I had, I would have brushed the hair from her face, cradled her face in my hand and then kissed her, and kissed her for a long time so that she knew my love for her. But this was just an uncontrolled act, I could not help myself, it was more of a tribute towards the perfection of her female form, to be unable to prevent myself from wondering what that soft touch, that gentle caress would feel like, my fingers, my touch on her buttocks, her soft slender skin, I just had to know. I got up, I rose to my feet, and Flower remained as she was. I left the bathroom to go forth to the living room and my chair. I was drawn to her, she was like a siren, but not through any act, not by flirting or chasing or behaving outrageously, I had been drawn in by her, as she was, lying naked in the bath tub, completely naked, her guard was down, she completely relaxed, and I could see the beauty within her, shining through the rest of her, it was unmistakeable, it was perfect. She must have known she was beautiful, regardless of the fact that she was in her early forties and chasing men half her age, she was ungainly, clumsy and nothing special to look at. But one day someone would notice, someone would see the real her, behind the hairstyle, behind the funky clothes, they would look past her clumsiness and her brash behaviour, they would see her with her guard down, the real her, the her that wanted and deserved to be loved, and they would take her to their heart and keep her safe forever, just like she deserved.

*

She never mentioned the incident in the bathroom again, and neither did I, neither did any of us. It had not sullied our relationship, and I was glad for that, but deep down I knew it would not have. Had the one that reached over to caress her felt that it would end or change our special bond forever, then he would not have done so. He just wanted Flower to know how beautiful she was, there and then in that instant. As the weeks went by, a change came out in Flower as well, she seemed to be more at ease with herself. She was less uncomfortable around handsome young men for a start, chasing them in a less obvious fashion, and she also seemed more comfortable with finding herself in her surroundings. That hard edge that always seemed to cause her to trip and fall or bang her knee or elbow on something had found itself coming to the surface less and less, she was still the same, but in less of a way. She was less worried and stressed about being alone, and more at ease with letting things come her way rather than trying to force events to happen. I was happy for her, we all were, she seemed happier with herself.

*

We would soon be ready to leave, it was indeed time for us to go, to make a fresh start. Flower had seen to all the arrangements so far, and we were so close to being ready, Lin and I only had one more thing to do before we could go, but we would have to do it soon, and quickly, and we would have to do it without Flower knowing, because we were going to go without her.

Lin had done as I told her, she was busy getting ready in her room, but that was not a problem as flower was about to go out, we did not need long, we just needed her to leave the flat for a few minutes, just long enough for Lin and I to leave without causing suspicion. I had asked Flower to go down to the twenty four hour convenient store to get some milk for the morning, she had complained at first, saying how late it was and how dark and cold it was outside, that was until I told her that I did not want to go there first thing in the morning, that I wanted to wake up and have breakfast without having to go out into the rain, and getting soaked through as a result, as the forecast had mentioned early showers. She should have noticed something was amiss, she never went anywhere without me, and I certainly had never sent her off on an errand alone before, neither did she notice that I had referred to myself and my own need for tomorrow, didn't she remember that I would not be here tomorrow, that another would take my place? But I had thought about this, so I had decided to be stern and abrupt with her while speaking to her, in the hope that making her panic and getting her flustered would distract her. We were nearly found out as well, I had not expected Flower to go back into the bedroom once I had given her money for the groceries and had expected her to go out straight away in order to be back as soon as she could, but as she was about to leave she suddenly turned around and went back into the bedroom.

Flower was shocked at first, and she just stood in the doorway, she certainly did not expect to see Lin all dressed up. Lin was putting on a pair of tights, one foot on the bed while she rolled the tights up her leg. She was wearing a silk Chinese dress, one usually seen worn by waitresses in expensive Chinese restaurants, it was sky blue and gold. Lin could see the shocked look on Flowers face, and she just smiled and told her that she had bought a new dress and was just trying it on, she even gave a twirl as she asked flower if she liked it. Flower complimented her, although she was stumbling over her words to do so, she went over to the bedside table to pick up her scratch card, she had won ten dollars and wanted to claim it while she was getting the milk. When she came out of the bedroom I could feel her looking at me, as if she was trying to work out what was going on, I did not take any notice of her, I just sat in my chair pretending to look at a book about Cezanne until she left.

Once she had gone we had to act fast, I went over to the bedroom to check on how Lin was doing, she had finished her makeup and she was just putting her final earring in place, she told me she was ready, so I took her hand and headed to the door, I grabbed a long black coat and wrapped it around Lin, and put the door on latch, I had to leave it open for when Flower returned, I just hope that she would understand.

While Flower was finding prices for cheap flights to China, Lin and I were trying to come up with a way to get her a new passport. When Lin first came over to the States to see her boyfriend, she had not told him she was coming, she said that she wanted it to be a surprise for him. Initially he had told her that he would do his

78

best to get back to Vietnam with a new visa as soon as he could, but when a new visa did not materialise and the talk about him coming back died down gradually, Lin took it up for herself to do something about it. She was going to go and see him instead, she knew he had tried his best to get back to her, so now she was going to show him that she was also capable of showing her love for him by going all the way to America to see him. She had been saving up all of her money for a flight, and even had to borrow money from many of her friends until finally she had enough. As the months went by she did become increasingly worried, the frequent e-mails that she was getting from her boyfriend were becoming fewer and fewer, but she thought that he was just busy with his life in the States, and that he was working hard every day, and not able to write to her all the time. But everything would be ok once she arrived there, they would be together again, and they would be happy again. It was a long flight, and an uncomfortable journey to do by yourself, there was no one to talk to for the entire journey and Lin was very nervous and slightly travel sick the whole time. By the time she arrived in New York and had cleared immigration and had picked up her baggage she was exhausted, she would have preferred to have told her boyfriend she was coming, to have him pick her up at the airport, it would have been so much easier to just fall into his arms right now and let him take her to his home, where she could rest, relax and sleep. But no, she had to do this by herself, to show him how much she loved him, she had to do all the difficult parts herself, then he would know how much she loved him, he could see everything she went through to be with him. So she was out of the airport, but how could she get to his house, which bus did she need? Was the underground easier, would it take her closer? She thought a taxi would be too expensive, as he lived out of the city itself. She did not know who to ask, she could not speak English and once she had picked up her baggage and walked to the arrivals lounge she had lost sight of the few Vietnamese passengers that she had seen on her flight. In the end she walked over to one of the counters, she did not know what kind of counter it was, but it looked like they might have been supplying rental cars for people. She could only say hello to the lady behind the counter, and when she smiled back, Lin handed her a piece of paper, it was the address of where she wanted to go. Smiling, the lady told her where to go and pointed a few times with her arm, until she saw the confused look on Lin's face, so she decided to walk her over to the ticket counter where she could get a Coach ticket, she must have told the girl selling the tickets that Lin could not speak English, because a Coach driver came over to walk Lin to the depot where her Coach would leave from, and fair play to him for keeping an eye on her, as he quickly rushed over to stop her getting on the wrong coach, and when her coach did arrive he helped her on with her luggage and showed the driver the address on the piece of paper. He was a big burley fellow, a black man with a full face and fatherly grin. Lin did not usually show her feelings well, she was timid and shy, once he had shown her to her seat and he had begun to walk down the aisle, back to the row of coaches outside, Lin rushed down the aisle after him, tapping him on the shoulder, and when he turned around she gave him a great big hug, trying to squeeze as hard as she could, knowing that the big man would hardy feel the hug otherwise, he took great joy from this, and the laughing, smiling big man waved to her as the Coach pulled away. It was indeed a long journey, it took the coach well over two hours until the driver got up from his seat to where Lin was sitting and told her it was time to leave. She was not sure what to do next as she stepped down from the coach's steps, until she looked back up at the driver to see him pointing her in the direction of a Taxi, of course she must be close now, just a few minutes away perhaps, and if it was only a short taxi ride then it would not be too expensive either. Lin had tried to freshen up a little bit in the airport bathroom, taking the time to wash her face and brush her hair, to try and look a little less worn out by all the travelling that she had done, but the long coach ride where she was too afraid to fall asleep had worn her out once more, and she hoped that when she did finally arrive, that she would not look to bad. All of the houses that the taxi was driving past were enormous, with long wide drives, and there were plenty of giant trees everywhere. Lin had never seen houses so big, only in the movies, and only in American movies. After only fifteen minutes the taxi pulled into a long drive, where the garden leading up to the house resembled more of a park. Well this was it, she was finally here, it was still morning despite all the travelling, the sun was shining through the trees, but she was so tired, almost dead on her feet, she just had to wait a little longer, she just needed to compose herself until she waited for someone to answer the door. Someone did come, it was her boyfriend's mother, she had expected her to call for him, but she didn't she just shook her head while she talked, apart from his name, Lin did not understand anything else his mother was saying, so Lin tried again, she was so nervous, and had been trying to learn English before her trip, but the people here spoke so quickly she could not understand them, however she did manage a few words, and his mother did realise that Lin had just arrived from Vietnam, where while her son was there Lin had been his girlfriend. Finally but disapprovingly she ushered Lin inside, where she could sit on the settee, more talking resumed, of which Lin did not understand any of what was going on. Finally waving her arms in the air, her boyfriend's mother got up and walked off, she was gone a few minutes, going from room to room, until she returned with a pile of things, laying everything down on the coffee table, she then headed off to the kitchen before returning with a glass of juice for Lin. The first thing that was shown to Lin from the pile on the table was a map of America, her boyfriend's mother fist pointed to the east coast and to New York, then pointed to the west coast and to San Francisco and California, then traced her finger between the two quite a few times. Next was a photo of her son, he was receiving his High School diploma, then came a letter and a certificate that Lin did not understand, however the mother repeatedly pointed to the senders address, then to a University prospectus booklet, UCLA in California, that's when it dawned on Lin, he was not here, her boyfriend had done what his parents wanted him to do before he went off to Vietnam, what he had always talked about doing, he had gone to University. But this can't be right, he had planned to come back to Vietnam, he was not going to go to University for a few years, he had said that he wanted to see the world first. So why had he gone now? And without telling her? Why had he gone to university in California, that was the other side of the country, Lin could never afford to go there, it was too far away, most of her money had already gone, he had promised to look after her, she did not want anything from him, she just wanted to be with him every day.

Lin was numb with shock, she had spent all the money she had, after working for so long to save up so much, and when she got home she would have to work even harder to get a new job to pay back all of her friends, who had leant her money that they could not really afford to give either, she had been such a fool, she wanted today to be the happiest day of her life, why didn't she tell him she was coming, why did it have to be a surprise, look what had happened now, she felt lost. Lin had been starring at the empty juice glass on the coffee table, not realising that his mother was trying to speak to her until she was given a little shake on the shoulder, she turned to see her imitating a pregnant belly with her hands, moving both hands over her stomach as a sign of pregnancy, then Lin realised that she was being asked if she was pregnant, oh no, of course not, she was not pregnant, that is not why she had come all this way, this was terrible, is that what his mother thought. But she did not seem convinced and instead of reaching for the phone to call her son, she went to get the car keys. She and Lin sat in silence for the long drive back to the city, what would Lin do now? She did not know, should she stay in New York a while? After all she had come all this way, even without seeing her boyfriend she should still make the most of it, but how? She did not have much money, perhaps enough for a week's stay in a hotel, if it was a cheap one. Maybe she should just go home, and begin working straight away, the sooner the better to pay back everything she owed, and the harder she worked the more she could take her mind off this terrible nightmare. After falling asleep a few times in the car, Lin decided to leave the decision up to his mother, if she drove her to the airport then that was that and she would get on the plane and leave, but if she drove her to the city then she would stay a few days at least, she would leave it up to her, her next destination would tell her everything.

The traffic in the city was slow and it ground away, the car moved forwards a little at a time, the buildings and skyscrapers were enormous, Lin had never seen such a city, but all the roads were a grid, however could you find yourself again if you were lost? Driving along 42nd Street the car came to a stop near Central Station, not knowing where Lin wanted to go, her boyfriend's mother had brought her here thinking that this would perhaps be the best place to find her way to wherever she was going to go next. She refused the money that Lin had offered her for driving her there, and without getting out of the car or helping her with her luggage she drove off, back through the city, cringing at how close she had come to having a Vietnamese daughter, and shuddering at the thought that Lin had lied about there not being a child on the way.

Standing inside central station, Lin was not sure where to go next, should she walk along the busy street outside, looking for a cheap hotel, or should she catch the subway to somewhere else? But where though? She did not have any idea where to go? Suddenly there was large crashing sound, as Lin turned she could see that two people's suitcases had become entangled as they were pulling them along on their wheels, and as the bags collided they had crashed together into a heap on the floor. Turning back to look at her own bag between her feet, Lin was suddenly shocked to find that it was not there, it had gone! Someone had taken it while she was not looking, but how could that be? She only turned away for an instant, and her bag was right there, right between her feet. Looking around desperately, she could not see it anywhere, Lin suddenly began running around the station, it began to dawn on her how important her bag was, all of her things were in there, her passport, her flight tickets, the rest of her money, it was all kept safe and together, and now someone else had it, it was all gone! It was a futile effort, trying to search for the culprit or the bag, central station is huge, with exits and platforms in all directions, returning to the main entrance, Lin just stood in the centre of the room, all around her were stairs leading back up to the street, and archways to the train platforms, a sea of people milling around in every direction, and above her just high ceilings, elaborately painted, Central station swallowed her up in its enormity, and down, down, down she went, sinking fast.

*

It had not taken long to find out where to go, not once he got the word out. The triads had been looking for those responsible for the brothel murders, having four of their own butchered had scared them into thinking that a rival gang was trying to take over. Knowledge is everything and the Triads had to know who was behind this, who was responsible, who to go after, so tracking them down was easy, I just had to ask the right questions, until I found my lead, until I found someone who was looking for the right answers. It wasn't easy, but I finally tracked down who I was looking for. I had to be subtle, creeping out of the apartment while the girls were asleep. He thought he was meeting me because I had information about who murdered the three Triads, the Mama-san and all the clients in the brothel, they thought they were hunting me down, but they were wrong, I had a link to them now, to those higher up, to those responsible. It did not take long to beat it out of him, a low level street informant who peddles information always gives things up too easily, within minutes I knew where to go, I knew where the rest of the Triads were, I knew where to take Lin to get my money.

That was three days ago, since then, I was just planning, I bought three dresses for Lin, all the same Chinese style, with a slit up the side of the leg, and I let her try them on until she found the size that fit her best. The informant had to die of course, after beating him I slit his throat, I could not let him go back to the Triads, not after beating so much information out of him, he would only go back to the Triads to warn them. Luckily snakes like him are rarely missed, not for more than a few days anyway, those that deal in information are always hiding from someone, and if his body does show up, then the Triads would just think that someone finally caught up with him. I left his body in the alley, throwing his light frame into the dumpster after I took his wallet and watch. Behind the same dumpster was my bag, it was time to get out of these blood soaked clothes.

One other thing that my would be liaison to the Triads had given me was the keys to his car, this made things a lot easier as I had just planned on stealing one for the night. It was parked right outside the diner, Lin and I got in, and she drove us towards Chinatown. There is more than one group of Triads based in New York, and I had to find just the right one, I had to make sure that they were not only involved in prostitution, but also in trafficking, human trafficking, and that they would buy Vietnamese girls as well, that was the most critical point. Some of the gangs only dealt with the Chinese, but the Triads that I was after, the ones that took

Flower, they would traffic anybody, and as it happens they had recently bought a Vietnamese girl, that was good news for us, I had found what I was looking for. At the desk, I used the little Mandarin that I knew, the fat balding man who was sat there, wiped his glasses on his shirt, then got up and beckoned me to follow. Lin and I walked behind him through the pool hall, our business wasn't there, we needed to go upstairs, to the office, walking through the dimly lit room, filled with cigarette smoke, Lin turned quite a few heads, I had hoped she would, she needed to look the part tonight. The office was like a penthouse suite, it was a stark contrast to the gloomy room below. There were three leather sofas dominating the room, and one wall had a circular window installed over an enormous fish tank, that was the length of the wall. There were three smaller rooms, but the only exit was through the double doors that we had come in, directly above the stairs. Leaving us to our business, the balding man returned to the pool hall downstairs, leaving Lin and myself with five others. We quickly got down to business, I wanted to know how much I could get for Lin, they would have to pay extra I argued, seeing how I brought her here and that they did not have to smuggle her into the country, they could see firsthand how beautiful she looked, she would make them a lot of money, and they could see how she had already been broken in, she was not going to run or fight or cry, all the hard work was done, they just had to pay for her.

The deal was struck, and the Triad boss was happy to pay, I could tell which one was his right hand man by the way he sat on the leather sofa, lounging back, drinking whiskey on the rocks. The other three just grunts, low level Triads, nervous and shy in their boss's presence, too nervous to sit even. I sent Lin back to the car, she could get her bag, the boss laughed with me as I told him it was full of her sexy underwear, and as I had forgotten my cigarettes as well, she might as well go and fetch them for me. See how good she is, see how she listens, how she obeys, watch her hips move as she walks away to the door, shaking that arse, making that silk dress cling to her body. All the men were captivated by her, they were practically drooling. The boss broke the silence by sending one of his men to the office to get my cash, and I took the opportunity to go asking for the bathroom, I could not remember the Mandarin word I needed, turning to the skinniest guy closest to me, I kept pestering him until the boss sent him to show me where to go, that was good, as long as it wasn't his right hand man, I needed someone who was not quite so sharp, someone who would not see it coming. At the bottom of the stairs the gangster just pointed across the dark pool hall, that was no good, I did not know what he meant, you have to show me, I was losing my use of Mandarin with every passing second. Reluctantly we walked among the tables, when we got to the toilets I just kept repeating, 'Which one's the Men's which one's the Women's?' By the third time he pushed the door open and showed me, here on the left the men's, look that little picture of a man, it's not even written in Chinese, turning to face me, looking fed up, the last thing he expected was a trap, once the door closed behind me I pounced. He was easy to take down, I had pestered the lightest guy in the room for a reason, I needed to take him out quickly and quietly, and just as I thought, underneath his suit jacket was a pistol. Now there were only four left, I went back up the stairs and straight through the double doors, good the boss's right hand man was still sitting down, drinking whiskey, and no one had left the room either, I had been afraid of that, all I needed to do now was wait for the other guy to get back, the one with my money.

'That was fast, eager for your money I see, of course you won't get it until the girl gets back here, were not stupid.' At this the boss laughed at his own joke, and right on cue, his man returned from the back office, with a wad of cash in his hand, no time to wait. I drew the pistol and killed the bosses right had man first, he might have been drinking, but he was a killer, I could tell, the shots hit him in the stomach the chest and the head, the silence in the room was destroyed as the three shots ran up his body, his whiskey glass remained still and undisturbed on the low table, the ice slowly melting with the temperature of the room. Next to fall was the other Triad, it was an easy shot, he was looking at his dead comrade so I just shot him in the back of the head. The boss I took down by shooting him in the knee, before wielding the gun on the last man, the one sent to the office. 'You, I know you know the combination to the safe, open it now.' And that's why I needed him alive. His palms were sweaty, but he still managed to open the safe quickly, I thanked him and ten shot him in the forehead as he still knelt in front of the safe, I headed back to the office, grabbed the rest of my money from the coffee table, this was Lin's money, how much they thought she was worth, I would show them how much she was really worth. The boss was in agony, and shouting curses at me, threatening to track me down. I knelt next to him and whispered in his ear. 'This is for Flower' As I stood up, the boss screamed out, 'Who the hell is Flower?' Then I shot him three times in the face. 'Exactly.' He did not even know those he had harmed.

The pool room was deserted when I got downstairs, I could not be too careful though, I half expected someone to jump out of the dark and start shooting at me. I went to the Men's and shot the last Triad, I had knocked him unconscious earlier, but they all deserved to die. Heading out of the fire escape in the back of the room, there was Lin waiting for me in the car. As I jumped in, I could tell by the look on her face that she felt that I had taken long enough to get things done, she was nervous waiting out there in the alley, and she was jumpy all the way back home, but it was done now, there were no cops after us, we had gotten away. I had killed those responsible for abducting Flower, I knew that there were more members of the gang than those few that I killed tonight, but I did not have time to hunt them all down, I killed those responsible the first night I met her, and I killed their boss tonight along with a few others. We had more cash than we needed to start three new lives, and I had a Vietnamese passport for Lin, everything had worked well for us, we did all of this in one foul swoop.

Standing at the top of the stairs, I had paused before going into the flat, I looked at Lin, she was stunning in her dress, in her hand was the bag containing all of the money that we had taken tonight, to look at her you would never think she had just walked out of a bloodbath. I looked at the key to the flat that was in my hand, the metal Hornet mascot key ring glistened with the light from the bulb in the hallway. Would the flat be open? Would Flower still be there? I looked at Lin again, I was almost afraid to go in, well...here go's. Pushing against the door gently, the flat was still unlocked, the strong light from the living room was seeping into the hallway as the door slowly swung open inch by inch, then in we went.

Flower was furious with us when we got back to the flat, she was crying and shouting, and throwing things around. She thought we had left her for good. She came back to an empty apartment, the door was open, all the lights were on, but no one was home. At first she thought something had happened to us, so she got scared, then she remembered Lin getting dressed up and thought that the two of us had run off without her. She was shouting at Lin, then hitting me with both her hands balled up into fists, striking my arm, then beating her fists against my chest. I told her over and over again that I was sorry, then I told her to simply shut up. I had always given Flower a free reign, never telling her what to do, or bossing her around, but right now I needed to get her to settle down, and the sooner I did so the better. I told her that Lin was very shaken up and scared, and feeling that a violent and turbulent atmosphere in the flat was the last thing that the poor girl needed I had to calm Flower down.

What I needed was a stiff drink, walking over to the counter I laid out three shot glasses, then I went and poured each of us a shot of vodka. I drank mine down straight away, refilling the glass instantly, leaning against the counter, grasping the edge, with my back to the girls, I waited for one or both of them to come over for their drink, when they did not I drank down my second shot before walking over to the kitchen table with the bag of money and simply pouring all of its contents onto the tables surface. The money went everywhere, but that was good, I wanted Flower to see what we had been up to. I would tell her the rest later, explaining why she could not come with us, or be involved in any way. I needed Lin there with me because she was strikingly beautiful, she was a plain enough girl in her every day clothes, but once she got dressed up that's when people really took notice of her. She was also calm and serene, and I needed her to act that way, to stand there, letting the men eye her up, weighing up how much she was worth. Flower would have acted differently, had she been in Lin's place, knowing that these were members from the same gang of Triads that took her captive, then she would have been wild with fury and would have lashed out, I can imagine her now trying to claw and scratch at those responsible, and this would have invariably ended up in both of our deaths. The money spilled about all over the place, much to Flowers amusement, but at least she could see what we had been up to, and why we had gone and left her. I began picking up the money off the floor, and arranging it, putting it together and into bundles on the table. Then I said that the best was yet to come, showing Flower the Vietnamese passport, it would be easy to make an incision along the side of the photograph, pulling the old picture out and swapping the girl's picture with Lin's. It was always easier to sneak out of a country than to try and sneak into one. I could see that Flower was biting her lip, holding back her tongue, she was dying to continue shouting, I could see on her face that she did not feel that the amount of shouting that we had allowed her to do had been justified, she wanted to shout and scream some more, she was hurt inside, she had felt betrayed and alone. But looking at Lin, who was still standing next to the front door looking at her shoes, Flower slowly walked over to her and gently wrapped her arms around her.

I told Flower to go with Lin into the bedroom, to help her change, she had had a traumatic evening, even though she had not seen the killing she had heard the gunshots while she waited in the back alley with the engine running. After searching the office, I searched the other two rooms leading off from the office, apart from the smaller private office in the back, the one containing the safe, one room was a bathroom, the boss and his men obviously did not use the one downstairs, neither did they want me to use their bathroom either, the other room although it wasn't a bedroom, contained a large double bed with purple silk bed sheets, they would obviously have taken their turns with Lin once I had left, and although Lin never saw this room, and no one laid a finger on her, she knew by the looks on their faces what they would have done to her. Flower ran her a bath, they hugged for a long time, before Lin went into the bathroom, and Flower came back over to where I was. No one else had touched their vodka, so I kept drinking their shots and pouring a fresh round every time. I had to explain to Flower that we needed a passport, that I needed Lin to come with me to make the deal look more convincing, I was sorry that I had left her out of our plans, but I felt it was better this way, I did not want her worrying about us. She hit me on the chest one more time, and then we hugged, I held her for a long time in my arms, long enough to feel the tears seep through my clothing and against my skin.

*

Lin was lying on her back in bed, staring up at the ceiling, she was just laying there, the crook of her elbow bent, to allow her arm to support her head. Flower was still asleep, lying on her side, sleeping in her underwear, she used to sleep in a t-shirt, as Lin did now, but as the days and nights grew hotter, and as Lin's English improved, Flower had asked her if she minded her sleeping in her underwear, Lin did not mind at all, they were family now, and they were more than comfortable in each other's company. Sunlight was beginning to filter into the room, slowly lifting the dark haze, gradually allowing your eyes to see more and more of the room's detail. The noise of the traffic outside had not become noticeable yet, but even as it's noise and volume increased it would not bother the residents of the apartment. Nothing ever did. Flower gave a slight stir, a sudden and lost mumble escaped her pouting lips, its origin and meaning lost forever. Lin turned back to look at the ceiling, thinking back to how she had to sleep on the streets, how different it was out there compared to the warm and cosy apartment. When Lin's bag and possessions had been stolen she was lost, the city swallowed her up, and she would have perished had it not been for the kindness of strangers. Lin knew what she needed to do, but she had no means to achieve her goal. She had to get to the Vietnamese Embassy, they would help her there, they would know what to do, they could help her get home. They could get her a new passport, they could contact the airline to get her flight details, they would be able to contact her parents, if she needed to pay for a replacement ticket or new passport then her parents would be able to help her out, surely the Embassy had ways to do all of these things, they must have come across the same problems time and time again, they could take care of her, she would not have to worry anymore. But where was the Vietnamese Embassy? Lin had no idea, she did not know where to even begin looking. Would all the embassy's be in the same place, or would they be all over the city? Was there even a Vietnamese Embassy in New York? Lin had not thought to check before she came out here, there could not be one in every American city, but surely there would be one here, or perhaps it would be in Washington D.C? Or another nearby city, but how would she get there? Trying not to panic, Lin began to think about what to do next. She started walking, maybe she would be fortunate, maybe she would meet another Vietnamese person that could speak English, with this in mind Lin began rushing around the city, looking for a Vietnamese restaurant, but she had no luck, she could not find any, and apart from blindly walking around in the hopes of stumbling across one, she had no other way of locating one. She stopped to ask a police officer for help, but without being able to speak English, all the officer could do was smile and try to ask what was wrong. His smile was reassuring, but neither of them could get any closer to understanding one another, in the end he walked her to a cafe, she would not go in with him, but when he returned he handed her a sandwich in a wrapper and a hot coffee, one of the ones that you can take out with you, with a white plastic cap on top of the cup that kept the coffee warm. He kept trying to talk to Lin, she thought he was trying to get her to go to the station with him, but in the end she rushed off. Thinking back now made Lin laugh, she giggled slightly as she lay there in bed, she had run off, only to turn around a few paces later and had returned to the kind officer, where she gave him a hug and a kiss on the cheek. He had not expected that, and Lin had not expected his kindness and eagerness to see her safe. She should have gone with him, he could have found out where she was from, simply by showing her a map of the world, then all was needed was a single phone call to a translator, and all of Lin's worries would have been over. But Lin was not used to helpful police officers, she was used to men in uniform being corrupt, she was used to bribes and lazy or selfish police officers, she certainly would not have trusted a young handsome and helpful police officer in her own country. Lin had another brainwave, she now knew how to get to the Embassy, gripped with excitement she rushed into the first bookshop that she found, scanning the shelves until she found the travel section, her travel guide had been stolen along with her bag, but she could just find another one here, there was bound to be a map or an address for the Vietnamese Embassy in it. But to her dismay, all the books were in English, of course they were, how could she have been so stupid she thought, why did she get her hopes up, why didn't she stop to think that they would not sell any books in Vietnamese here. Lin was worn out by now, the stress of the day along with rushing around had exhausted her, she had spent the entire morning on a bus or in a car, and now she had run herself ragged around the city. It was getting dark, and Lin was running out of time, she was getting more and more panicked, she was getting scared. Spying some notebooks on a table Lin went over, maybe she could make people understand, maybe she should trust the police after all, the young officer had been nice, maybe the police really would be helpful. Great, Lin found what she was looking for, among the notebooks were many pens and felt tips, tearing a blank page from a notebook, Lin quickly set herself to work, drawing a star in the middle of the little palm sized page, then she coloured it in with a yellow pen, before finding a red marker, making a bold red flag, her flag, this must help her find her way home, it was her only chance. Walking quickly to the busy street where she had received a kind cup of coffee and some food, maybe her kind police officer would still be there, if not it was a busy street, she was sure to find another police officer. Lin had been scared of the police, she was tired and she had panicked, she thought that without her passport and visa documents on her then she would instantly be in trouble, and without bribe money then she would be in even deeper trouble, but now she thought that if she could just explain, then everything would be ok, and she could go home. Luckily Lin did not have to walk all the way back to where she was before, she had come across another police officer, he was of course a different officer, he was twice as wide as her and was middle-aged, with a big stomach, had it not been for the strength that was visible in his arms, then he would have reminded her of the fat officers she often saw in Saigon, but he was more like a bull, with no neck, and a wide back and shoulders. He was gruff and loud when he was talking to Lin, barking each word, he was far too aggressive in his manner, this did not make Lin comfortable at all, but she was going to continue to try, she held out the little hand-made Vietnamese flag, as if it were a business card, holding it with both hands for the officer to inspect, but he was not patient and hardly looked at the flag, he seemed to be berating Lin for wasting his time, Lin looked around, hoping to see another police officer nearby, the stout officer was still shouting at her, but she was not paying him any attention now, she was walking away, it would be dark soon, and she would need a place to stay, she would have to find somewhere to sleep, slipping the little flag into her green jacket pocket Lin walked off, residing herself to her fate, she was lost, well and truly lost, in a world that did not understand her she found herself stranded and alone.

That had been her first night in the city, Lin did not know where to go to sleep, everywhere seemed too busy, should she seek a quiet alley, or an empty park to sleep in? Or would that be too dangerous? Was it safer around people or was it safer alone? She did not know, should she try and find other homeless people, and spend the night next to them? Maybe they would be angry with her, or maybe the police would be angry with her if she was caught sleeping far away from where the homeless lived, how could she find them anyway? Her walking had brought her to a small church only a few blocks from Central Park, she had thought of sleeping in the park, but then felt that it was too big, and that scared her, the church was on the corner, and there were expensive looking clothes shops next to it, maybe this would be a good place, she could sleep in the churchyard, beneath the great shadows of its trees, if she got scared then she could huddle next to the wall, hiding herself from the street, and in the daytime she could just sit on the wall, she had already passed the same church earlier and had seen many people sitting and eating on its walls, so she thought that it was ok to do so, no one would prevent her from being here. Lin buried her head in her hands, taking a deep breath in, before letting out the same slow deep breath.

Looking back, Lin counted herself lucky, she was safe here, she had friends now, although they were strange, they were her family. They trusted her before they even knew her, they treated her kindly, they kept her warm and safe, and they never asked for anything in return. Flower was like a big sister, or perhaps more accurately more like the aunt of the family, acting like the kind of aunt that wanted to shrug the stigma of age that came with that title, thinking themselves to be too young and free spirited, pretending to be your cousin or sister instead. He had even begun calling Flower 'Auntie', but to Lin she would always be her sister, her big sister that took care of her. He also took care of Flower, he took care of both of them, but who was he, the man with no name, the collector of strays. As far as Lin knew even Flower did not know his name, he was an enigma. He was their benefactor, but a benefactor without a name or a title, but that was up to him, maybe he wanted to be a ghost, maybe having something as solid as a name would anchor him to this world, maybe that is what he was afraid of? He took care of all of the bills, not that Lin ever even saw a bill, she did wonder what was the arrangement with the rent, was there a landlord or landlady or did this apartment, or flat as he liked to call it, belong to him? Certainly every time they went out he paid for everything, not that they had much choice, neither Flower nor Lin had a job, but he did not seem to want them to work either, Lin seemed to think that he liked having them around all day.

Lin reached up and took the little Vietnamese flag off the wall, the room did not have many decorations, so she had stuck it up there, her little contribution, lying back on the bed, turning her flag over and over, revealing the blank side beneath, then back to the golden star atop a red field, over and over the flag turned in her hands, flipping from a blank page to her own handiwork on that cold lost day. Suddenly she remembered something her Grandfather had taught her when she was a child; she had seen a small badge in a market and had asked her grandfather about it, wanting to know which country it was from, the week before she had been learning about flags in school, and she was proud to recognise her flag and point it out to her Grandfather every time she saw it. But she was shocked to hear that the little badge was Vietnamese as well, there was the same gold star, but behind it was half red and half blue, not at all what she had learnt about in school. She was about to accuse her Grandfather of teasing her when he explained that during the American war this flag had also been used by the Vietcong, but now that the whole country belonged to the Vietnamese, the entire flag could be red, as it should be. Maybe this is what he is like, not quite one thing, not quite the other, torn between two worlds, maybe he is also in a state of flux, in a transitional period, waiting to be whole again, maybe he is the half red and half blue flag. It was then that Lin decided to give him her little red flag, for him to have and to keep as his own, who knows it might prove to be his talisman, it might lead him the way, it might take him home.

*

So this was it, the beginning of the journey, it was going to be a long one, but worth it in the end, for the sake of the three of us, we were going away, away from here to start again, a new world a new life. The Airplane seat felt strange, I had never been on a plane before, I began to feel myself wondering if it would be comfortable for all those hours? I thought to myself that it would have to do, therefore there was no point in thinking about it any longer. The plane began moving along the runway, I realised that I had been very selfish, perhaps the girls were afraid of flying, I should have been thinking about them and not about myself. I put down the book I was reading, pausing to finger the bookmark, a handmade flag of Vietnam that Lin had made once, and had given to me. I turned to the girls, Flower was sat to my left, and Lin was on my right, they both looked fine, perhaps they were used to flying, or maybe they just hid their fears well. The three of us smiled at each other and I took them each gently by the hand as the plane began to ascend. Once we had levelled out, and the cabin crew were walking up and down the aisles handing out refreshing hot towels and boiled sweets, Flower leant into her hand luggage and pulled out a white baseball top and handed it to me. It was brand new, and I had no idea how she got it. 'It's China's baseball team, it's the national uniform. You see the Chinese flag on the sleeve, and it has a bit of red here and there too, a bit more colour for you to wear, and now you will blend in, you will look less like a tourist.' Yes I could see the little flag on the sleeve, I could also read 'CHINA' in large letters on the front, I doubted that wearing this would make me look less like a tourist, but perhaps the locals would see how much I appreciated their country if they saw me wearing this shirt, maybe they would appreciate that. It was a really nice shirt, and I thanked Flower for it, she must have gone to a lot of trouble to get it for me, I did not want to think how much it cost her. Leaning across me she told Lin not to worry, flower had not bought anything for her, as she was waiting for them to go shopping together in Beijing. Flower told her that there would be plenty of beautiful clothes for them to buy, and that she would look stunning in a Chinese silk dress, well Lin and I already knew that much, but Flower did not seem to notice her error, so we let it pass. They were happy to be going to China, they were excited and they could barely contain themselves. I swapped seats with Flower so that the two of them could continue talking without having me in their way, I returned to my book, and whenever I did not have to turn the page, I held Flower's hand with my right hand. Although she had turned away from me to continue speaking with Lin, she gripped my fingers with her small hand, stroking them with her thumb in a continuous and rhythmical fashion, as a Mother would soothe a child, or a lover would caress her partner.

We had spent many hours discussing our future, Flower had come up with the plan to go to China, we could all be safe there she said. It would be her turn to look after us, she kept saying. That was fine with me, I was looking forwards to it, it would be a fresh new start, but I wondered if it was what Lin was hoping for? We had managed to get out of America without any problems, once we were in China we could help Lin get safely back to Vietnam and to her family if that is what she wanted. We would even deliver her right to her front door, we would not dream of having it any other way, we certainly could not leave her at the airport and wave her off. We would make whatever journey she wanted with her, the three of us together. Lin had told us that she had used up all of her savings, and had had to borrow a lot of money, well that would not be a problem, I still had enough money, well we all did, Lin helped me rob the Triads and I would use that money to pay back all of her family and friends. Lin wanted to see her family again so much, we would have to take her there once our Vietnamese visas were sorted out, of course once Lin was back in Vietnam she would have to pretend that she had recently lost her passport in order to get another one, she certainly could not use the stolen one more than a couple of times. Her family wanted to see her so much, Lin had often called them from the States, and it would not be long before we would leave China to go to Vietnam together. I would like to think that Lin might come back to us to Beijing soon, I hope when we see the city Lin will want to come back. If not, at least she is not too far away, and we would always be thinking of her.

Flower and Lin did finally find out a little bit more about me a few days ago, it was after we had gotten Lin a replacement for her lost passport, we were busy filling out forms for our Chinese visas when suddenly Flower panicked and started talking in a very hurried fashion to Lin, it wasn't until the both of them came over to me that I realised what all the fuss was about. Flower had her passport back, and we were going to try and get Lin into China with a different passport, but the girls wanted to know what we would do about my passport. Well I told them that was not a problem, seeing that I already had mine hidden safely with all of the cash on top of the wardrobe. This left the girls flabbergasted, I have never seen Flower speechless before, and even the calm and quiet Lin was shocked enough to let her mouth drop open. Both the girls rushed back into the bedroom to drag the bag down, carrying it together and dumping it on the kitchen table, and there in Flowers hand was my passport. I had never told the girls my name before, I had never needed to use it. It's true I remembered what it was, but it always felt like a different side of me, like looking into the past. But now the girls knew my name, my age and where I was from. My accent, and apparent lack of an American accent had always driven Flower crazy. Both girls had always wanted to learn more about me and my past, and although I never cared or showed the slightest interest, they were very keen to find out about my past, where I had come from, who I really was, why I was in New York. But to me all this was just meaningless knowledge, even if I remembered all these things, or learnt them again it would not change me, I would still live my life the way I did. I had a feeling that now Flower had something to go on, something solid about my past, now she would use that as a solid anchor to gain more information about me, well I would not mind, it would seem to make her happy, and I could see it becoming a pet project for her, but even if she did find my home or my family, these things did not interest me, and I doubted that I would do anything about them. I will just let her do her own thing, whatever made her happy, and then leave it at that, the past is the past.

Flower had been helping me, teaching me how to think differently, she was trying to open new doors for me, I don't know if it was working, but if was definitely helping. She had said that when we get to China, she does not want to hear any more crazy talk from me anymore, I had to talk about myself in the first person and not as a plural either. There may be many of us, but for now one will do, that's what she had said, and I still grin to myself as I remember her standing in the kitchen with her hands on her hips, telling me off like some old aunty. I had been calling her 'Aunty' for a while now, and the nick-name had stuck, it suited her and after all from now on it would be her that would look after Lin and me, and all the other me's to come when we were living in China. It would be a shock to begin with, saying that it's a culture shock is an understatement, we would have to begin again, learn our way around, our way of life would be different, we would have to find our own routine. But we would be fine, all of us, they might not like me, for what I have done, but this is the hardest part, today sitting on this plane, the rest would have to work it out as best they could, pioneer a whole new world, one day at a time. Flower seems to think that I will get better out there, she keeps saying that over and over again, she seems to think that one day, in the end there will only be one of us left, I will wake up one day and not die that night,

104

but continue to wake every single day, one of us, the lucky one, will continue to live in this body for ever, and not have to share it anymore, that would be nice, to have a home, to own your own home, your body, your sanctuary, to close your eyes and hold yourself close and feel your soul deep, deep inside of you, warm and dry in there, in the dark, knowing that you are protected from the outside world, to know this and allow yourself to smile, just a little. Perhaps it will be me, maybe I am the lucky one, but I think not, there will be too many changes, there are difficult times ahead, but maybe soon, that time will come, when all is well again, and we are settled in Beijing, and Lin is safe back in Vietnam, or with us, where ever she wants to end up in the end, maybe one day as the sun rises, so will I, and my life will survive the twilight and the setting sun, to endure many more sunsets to come.

About the author

Andrzej Griffith was born in Bangor in Wales.
Paper Man is his first book.
He currently resides in the Llŷn Peninsula in North Wales.

Published in 2013 by FeedARead.com Publishing –
Arts Council funded

A CIP catalogue record for this title is available from
the British Library.

Lightning Source UK Ltd.
Milton Keynes UK
UKOW04f0420071213

222549UK00001B/19/P